W9-DGK-932

May 7, 1962
Brenda Gladfelter
1892 Marigold Rd.
York, Pa.

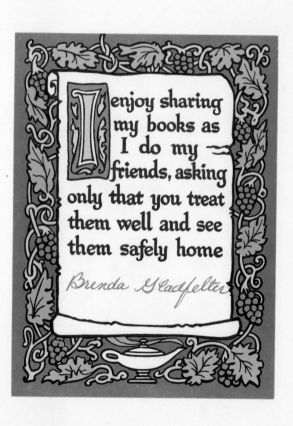

I enjoy sharing my books as I do my friends, asking only that you treat them well and see them safely home

Brenda Gladfelter

Champlain Summer

CHAMPLAIN SUMMER

Marjorie Vetter

Funk & Wagnalls Company   New York

The author is grateful to the following for their courtesy in allowing the reprinting in this book of the copyrighted material listed below:

Mrs. Arthur Guiterman for the poem "Vergennes, Vermont," by Arthur Guiterman.

G. P. Putnam's Sons for the poem, "The Wreck of the Julie Plant," from *Poetical Works* by William Henry Drummond.

Contents

With memories of many happy Champlain Summers,
I dedicate this book to my sister and brother
DOT and BILL BUNN
whose Lake Champlain summer cottage was commandeered
by the Turners for the duration of this story.

Champlain Summer

No Glamour for Kit

The door of the subway car rolled slowly shut and the train jerked ahead. Kit Turner, tense with the strain of urging the lurching, rattling monster on its way, looked at her watch for the third time since she had boarded the train two stations back.

Why had she allowed herself to be persuaded to play tennis after school? Of course she had had time enough for a set, or perhaps even two, cutting it fine. If she had not lost the second set through stupid carelessness, she would never in the world have let Susan Carter prevail upon her to play a third set. At the time, nothing had seemed so important as making up for her mistakes and taking that third set.

Now she wondered why she had ever thought beating Susan mattered. When she had picked up her watch to put it on after her shower, she had discovered with horror that her mother had already been waiting for some time to meet her at Lord & Taylor's. Kit hadn't money enough for a taxi, and it would take at least forty-five minutes for her to get there by subway.

Naturally her mother would be angry. Who could blame

her? And today of all days, when Kit had hoped tactfully to win the point she had been arguing all week. Mrs. Turner was determined to buy her daughter a new party dress for the summer activities at Lake Champlain, where the Turners had a cottage to which they were soon to go for the summer. But Kit wanted none of it. She had hoped, if she caught her mother in an indulgent mood, to wangle a new tennis racquet in place of the dress she dreaded to own. To be an hour late to begin with made the prospect of success pretty dim.

When the train finally ambled into Grand Central Station, Kit was the first to step from the car. She sprinted up the stairs and as she ran toward Fifth Avenue she looked at her watch again. It was five minutes to four. She was an hour late, all right. Her mother might have given up waiting and gone home in disgust. At best, Kit could hardly expect her to be in a very good humor.

Zigzagging across and downtown with the traffic lights, she streaked across Fifth Avenue the minute the green light flashed and charged through the doors of the department store. As she stepped off the elevator at the Young New Yorker Shop, her mother came toward her.

"Katharine! Where in the world have you been?" Mrs. Turner's voice was sharp.

"Oh, I know, I know," Kit said hurriedly. "You must be frantic. I'm so sorry."

"But what happened?" her mother persisted. "What could have made you a whole hour late?"

"You're going to be awfully mad." Kit hesitated and then blurted out, "I was playing tennis with Sue and I didn't watch the time."

"Playing tennis!" Mrs. Turner echoed in outrage. "Katharine Turner, I could shake you." She looked as if she might put her words into action. "I wanted to get back early this afternoon because I don't like to leave Aunt Charlotte alone too long, and your father expects to get home for dinner this evening."

"I'm sorry," Kit mumbled again.

"Do you realize how inconsiderate it is for you to keep me waiting like this while you fool around playing tennis? You're old enough to have some sense of responsibility."

"I know, I know," Kit said again. "I'm really sorry." After a little pause, she ventured meekly, "Couldn't we just forget about the dress and go home? It's so late, and with Dad coming home . . . and Aunt Charlotte—and everything. I keep telling you I honestly won't need a party dress at the lake this summer, especially since Marge and Babs won't be there."

"Katharine Turner! Don't tell me you did this on purpose!" her mother exclaimed in exasperation.

"Mother!" Kit looked hurt. "Of course not. It's just—well, you know how I hate parties. I don't want you to spend your time and money on a silly dress I'll never wear."

"This nonsense has gone far enough. I came downtown especially to buy this dress for you and I'm going to do it. I meant what I said last night. I don't care how many swimming races or tennis matches you win so long as you go to some parties too. Deliver me from these athletic women who haven't any charm or poise or social sense. I don't propose to bring up my daughter to be one."

Kit didn't dare mention the tennis racquet as she followed her mother into the dress shop. She stood silent while Mrs.

Turner talked with the saleswoman and displayed no interest as several dresses were held up for inspection. Mrs. Turner said nothing, but she looked again as if she felt like giving her daughter a good shake.

"What do you think?" she demanded at last. "The pink is pale enough not to clash with your hair. The white is sweet and the aqua is rather stunning. Do you want to try them?"

Kit agreed without enthusiasm. She tried the white and then the pink with indifference. Her mother was right. The white was sweet, full, and girlish—and completely sickening, Kit thought. The pink, though the shade was just right to be effective with Kit's red-gold hair, was not at all becoming in style.

When Kit put on the aqua dress her mother and the saleswoman exclaimed together in delight. The straight lines of its simple cut emphasized the rounded grace of her lovely figure, while the green blue brought out the whiteness of her skin and deepened the blue of her eyes.

"It's perfect, Kit." Mrs. Turner's annoyance was forgotten in her pleasure at the picture Kit made. "You look lovely. Do you like it? Shall we take it?"

Kit was puzzled by her own reaction. She could not fail to see that the dress was becoming. The figure in the mirror was distinctly—she fumbled for a word and came up with alluring. Suddenly she looked grown-up and completely feminine. It was a jolt to find that this pleased and excited her.

The feeling was momentary, soon quenched by her distaste for the parties to which the dress would commit her. She turned to her mother.

"It *is* pretty," she conceded, "but honestly, Mother, I don't

want it. I don't really need it and I feel—well—silly in it."
This last was not strictly true. She did not, at that moment,
feel at all silly, but she had not yet learned to be at ease
socially in a new and grown-up world, and the prospect of
having to wear the dress to the formal functions for which
it was designed dismayed her.

Tagging after her good-natured older brother, Ken, from
the time she could toddle, Kit had learned to ride, ski, play
baseball, football, and hockey like a boy. She had always
found boys more satisfactory playmates than girls and she
could hold her own with them in any sport.

When Ken had entered high school and girls had begun
to call him on the telephone, hang around the playing field
when he was practicing with the football or baseball teams,
and walk by the apartment where the Turners lived, Kit
had been at first amused and then disgusted. As Ken had
begun to fuss over the way his slacks were pressed, the fit of
his jackets, the color of his ties, she had been puzzled and
scornful.

She couldn't help overhearing his end of the lengthy, inane conversations which he carried on with one or another
of the popular girls he dated. It all seemed pretty stupid to
Kit, unable to comprehend why Ken wanted to waste his
time in such a ridiculous way.

At twelve and thirteen, when her friends and classmates
in their turn had begun to giggle and whisper and tease
each other about boys, and to flutter and pose and try to
attract their attention, even to call them on the telephone
and regard them generally as strange and wonderful beings,
Kit had been baffled and uneasy.

She couldn't see anything remarkable or awe-inspiring

about grubby, gangling boys with changing voices whom she could beat at tennis. Even now at fourteen she still felt the same way.

"What is the matter with you, Kit?" Mrs. Turner said now with the note of exasperation back in her voice. "How can you possibly feel silly in a simple, extremely becoming dress?"

"I know I'm an idiot," Kit said uncomfortably, "but I hate the kind of parties you'd wear a dress like this to. I'm just no good at dating and dancing and small talk with boys."

"Nonsense," said her mother unsympathetically. "You'll find all that comes naturally with a little experience."

It was all very well for her mother to talk that way, Kit thought. She had been one of the three beautiful Duryea sisters of Virginia about whom young men had hovered in droves. She had been a belle and loved every minute of it, and she wanted the same sort of thing for her daughter.

It seemed to Kit that her mother must have been born beautiful, charmingly feminine, exquisitely poised. Though Kit had inherited Mrs. Turner's small bones and good figure, she looked like her father. She had his red-gold hair, sandy brows and lashes, his wide mouth with the small even white teeth, his white skin that burned and blistered and burned again—and never, never tanned.

She used no make-up and thought of herself as sandy-haired and unattractive, when she bothered to think of her looks at all. Usually she was much too busy with various extra-curricular activities, among which sports ranked highest, to give such matters any consideration at all.

"We will take the aqua dress," Mrs. Turner told the saleswoman. "Will you charge and send it, please?" She motioned to her daughter. "Hurry along, Kit, and change as quickly as possible."

"It's too bad Marge and Babs won't be at the lake this summer," Mrs. Turner said to Kit above the noise of the subway as they rode uptown. "You'll miss them of course, but maybe there'll be some new girls to take their places. The Gunnersons have rented their house, I understand."

"I hope there'll be someone young in the family," Kit said, "so we can use the tennis courts. I'd hate to have to go all the way down to the club every time I wanted to play."

"For your sake, I hope so too," Mrs. Turner agreed. "But remember, have all the tennis and riding and water skiing you want, but no squirming out of a single evening party."

It was going to be a honey of a summer, Kit thought wryly as they went up the stairs at their station, if her mother stuck to this business of insisting that Kit go to the stupid parties, club dances, and all that sort of stuff. Much as she looked forward each year to the time she spent at the lake, she was worried that she might find it lonely this year because her special friends, Marge Gunnerson and Babs Wheaton, would not be there.

The Gunnersons, whose land adjoined the Turners' on the east, had rented their large and luxurious summer home and gone abroad. The Wheatons were spending the summer with Mrs. Wheaton's family in Canada. The Wheaton cottage, which was small but modern and very attractive, had not, so far as Kit knew, been rented.

At the top of the stairs a nondescript yellow dog with a pointed nose and a long waving tail came running up to

Kit. "Hi, fella," she greeted him and stooped to pat him. He wriggled all over with pleasure, and Kit could not resist stopping to pat him again.

Mrs. Turner continued walking rapidly on her way home to various duties for which Kit's tardiness had made her late.

The yellow dog followed Kit, looking up at her with his heart in his big brown eyes.

"You're just a poor old stray, aren't you, boy?" Kit said lovingly. "No collar, no license. I wish I could take you home."

"Come along, Kit," Mrs. Turner urged impatiently. "We're late enough now. I need you to help me with dinner."

Kit waved the yellow dog away sternly, ordering him about his business, but he thought it was a game and came bounding joyously back again. She knew that this was not the afternoon to ask a favor of her mother, but she heard herself saying, "Couldn't I keep him, Mom? He's only a stray. Oh, Mom, couldn't I, please?"

Mrs. Turner stopped her fast walk abruptly. "Are you out of your mind, Kit? How many times do I have to tell you that it's unfair to keep a dog shut up in an apartment?"

"I'd take him out," Kit said, "and he could sleep in my room. I'd take all the care of him, really I would."

"Judging by the sense of responsibility you displayed today," her mother said coldly, "I'd probably be walking a dog three times a day."

Kit had said she was sorry over and over. Couldn't her mother let it go at that and forget it? Did she have to keep bringing it up for the rest of the day? Grownups were so unsympathetic, so un-understanding. One little slip, and they made a mountain of it.

Kit walked along, nursing hurt feelings in silence, while the yellow dog frisked at her heels. He certainly was full of play. Thank goodness he didn't look thin and hungry. Maybe he belonged to someone in the neighborhood and had run away. That would explain his not wearing a collar with a license. If she could keep him for only a few days, maybe she could find the owner. She tried again. "Couldn't we take him in for a few days while I try to find the owner?"

"Have you forgotten we leave for the lake this weekend?"

"I bet he'd love it up there."

"No doubt," Mrs. Turner agreed drily, "but how do you plan to get him there?"

Kit saw their car "packed to the gunwales," as her father put it, for every trip to the lake. This time there would be an extra passenger, for Mrs. Turner's Aunt Charlotte had come up from Virginia to spend the summer with them at the lake. No, there would be no room for a yellow dog. Spartan-like, Kit shooed the animal away, slipped through the apartment house door, and shut it quickly behind her. She followed her mother into the elevator, thinking dolefully that for the first time in her life she was not looking forward to summer at Lake Champlain.

One More Complication

"Well! Home are the wanderers at last," Aunt Charlotte said tartly, putting down her book, as Mrs. Turner and Kit entered the living room. "I was beginning to think you'd been kidnaped."

"I'm sorry we're so late," Mrs. Turner apologized. "I hope you weren't too lonely."

"It *was* rather a long afternoon all by myself," Aunt Charlotte replied crisply. "I was thankful I had a good book." She glanced significantly at the clock. "I would have been glad to start preparations for dinner if I had known what to do."

Even more than Sally Belle Turner, Aunt Charlotte had been a beauty. You could tell that, Kit had thought the first evening of her visit, by the way she took masculine homage for granted even now. With her slim figure, erect carriage, her lovely white hair and expressive eyes, she was still lovely to look at. She knew it, and expected deference and attention.

"Thanks, Aunt Charlotte," Mrs. Turner said. "It was good of you to think of it, but there was really nothing for you to do. I'll get things under way just as soon as I take off my hat. Kit will help me."

"You're not going to shut me off in the living room like a guest," Aunt Charlotte protested. "Let Katharine set the table. I'll help you in the kitchen. I'm family, not company, you know."

When Kit had put away her hat, bag, and gloves, combed her hair and washed her hands, she went into the dining room.

"Place mats or tablecloth?" she called to her mother in the kitchen.

"Your father will be home for dinner for the first time in four days, so let's make it a party. Use the écru cloth and the Limoges china," Mrs. Turner answered. "Dick didn't call, did he?" she asked Aunt Charlotte a little uneasily.

"Two calls for Ken, that's all," Aunt Charlotte said, and at that moment the telephone rang. It was Miss Westley, Mr. Turner's secretary, to report that Mr. Turner was sorry he would be delayed about an hour, but if they wanted to wait, he thought he could be there for dinner.

"I was afraid Dick was going to be stuck downtown all evening," Mrs. Turner said with relief as she rang off. "He's coming, but he'll be late. That's all right. We won't have to rush so now."

Kit spread the écru cloth carefully, replaced the crystal circle of green fern and anemones in the center of the table and flanked it with pink candles in silver holders. This was one of the few feminine tasks she enjoyed. She liked to make an attractive picture of the table. She was placing the crystal goblets carefully in their proper positions when she became conscious of the conversation her mother and Aunt Charlotte were carrying on in the kitchen.

"How pleased you must be, Sally Belle, that Ken is doing so well in his studies," Aunt Charlotte was saying. "He seems to be popular too, judging by the number of telephone calls he receives. But what about Katharine? She has no calls from boys at all. Doesn't she have any beaux?"

"Katharine is only fourteen," Mrs. Turner answered. Kit thought her mother needn't sound quite so defensive. "She keeps so busy with school and sports, she hasn't yet given much thought to boys as beaux."

"She really isn't unattractive," Aunt Charlotte said consolingly. Kit could imagine the sympathetic look she was bestowing on a niece with the bad luck to have an unpopular daughter. "Never you mind, Sally Belle, honey," she added tactfully, "it may be she's the kind to blossom late."

"Just a case of arrested development," Kit thought with a grimace, and added mentally in imitation of Aunt Charlotte's soft, sweet voice, "Don't worry, Katharine honey, you'll grow up one of these days."

She was placing the china on the table as Ken came in. "Where's Mom? How soon is dinner?" he asked in one breath, as he usually did each evening when he came home.

"Mom's in the kitchen," Kit told him. "Dinner's not till eight because Dad will be late."

"I'm starved." Ken bolted out to the kitchen and Kit could hear him greeting his mother and Aunt Charlotte and demanding food to sustain him until dinner.

"Any calls, Mom?" she heard him ask as the refrigerator door slammed.

"No you don't," Mrs. Turner squealed. "Put that pie right back. It's for dessert, and don't you dare touch it."

"Two young ladies called," Aunt Charlotte said. "Their names and telephone numbers are on the desk pad."

"Thanks, angel, you're a lovely lady." There was a little scuffling noise as if Ken had given Aunt Charlotte a bear hug. She protested, laughing, but her voice sounded pleased. "How about a glass of milk, Kenneth, and a piece of the cake we had for lunch? That would be all right, wouldn't it, Sally Belle?"

"You're as kind as you are beautiful, Aunt Charlotte, and no man could ask for more," Ken said, and Kit could hear the refrigerator door open and shut, more quietly this time, as Aunt Charlotte waited on her great-nephew.

Ken could tease Aunt Charlotte and she loved it, Kit thought enviously. She would never dare squeeze her dignified great-aunt or laugh and joke with her as Ken did. She was really afraid of Aunt Charlotte, she admitted honestly. She found such queenly bearing and complete assurance formidable, but Ken was not awed.

Her task completed to her satisfaction, Kit went back to her room to look over her lesson assignments for the next day. They were not heavy in this last week before vacation. When she had made quick work of them, she picked up a book in which she became so engrossed that she did not hear her father come in, and she had to be called twice for dinner.

Mrs. Turner was serving the dessert when the telephone rang. Ken excused himself to answer it, but it was not for him this time. He called his mother to the telephone. "Mrs. Lester," he said, as he resumed his place.

In a lull in the conversation at the table, Kit could hear

her mother's side of the conversation. "Why, Adele, how wonderful!" Pause. "When did you . . . ?" Pause. "Fine. See you later."

"Well, what do you think of that?" Mrs. Turner asked the company in general, as she came back to the table. "The Lesters have rented the Wheaton cottage for the summer."

"Oh, no!" Kit groaned. "Elaine for the whole summer. I can't bear it."

"Nonsense," said her mother, "it will be very pleasant for you to have Elaine in the Wheaton cottage. She'll help to fill Marge's place."

"Mother!" Kit's protest was vehement. "Elaine could never take Marge's place. She'll just complete the utter ruin of my summer, that's all."

Mrs. Turner, repeating her telephone conversation to her husband, paid no attention to Kit. "They're coming over this evening to talk about it," she ended. "We'll have to hurry."

Kit had known Elaine all her life, but there had never been any love lost between them. Elaine was dainty and feminine with a fragile Dresden China prettiness the boys seemed to find especially appealing. She was a year older than Kit, and whenever Kit saw her in the halls at school, she had some boy or other bending adoringly over her.

Elaine had always been what Aunt Charlotte called "a little lady." When they were very small, Kit had chewed her bonnet strings, scattered her cookie crumbs prodigally all over herself and her carriage, squirmed and wriggled until she and her pillow were a rumpled mess. Elaine had sat up straight, cool and fresh and unwrinkled.

"Why can't you behave like Elaine?" Mrs. Turner and visiting aunts and grandmothers were constantly demanding.

Elaine, staying with the Turners at the lake, had played sweetly with dolls in the shade of the porch, while Kit skinned her knees climbing trees. Elaine had raised her dainty eyebrows when Kit, hot and dirty, had trudged down from the Armstrong farm in the wake of Ken and his friends, boasting that she had milked three and a half cows. Elaine splashed about, squealing, near the shore, while Kit made even Ken, the best swimmer in the group, extend himself to outdistance her.

Kit had pitched such a neat curve that the boys had been glad to have her on their team. None of the boys in Ken's crowd had ever bothered with Elaine then. But now they fell all over themselves, Kit thought wryly, to carry her books, date her for dances.

"My vacation will be ruined—completely ruined," Kit moaned again dramatically. "How can I stand having 'Elaine the fair, Elaine the lovable, Elaine, the lily maid . . .' next door to me all summer? One week used to be bad enough. But all summer . . . !" She held her head, groaning.

3

The Lake at Last

"What's the idea?" Kit grumbled to herself in disgust. "This is an outrageous hour to wake up the very first morning."

She knew instantly where she was, even before she opened her eyes, though the Turners had only reached their summer cottage around midnight the night before. They were late this year. Their plans to arrive a week earlier had been spoiled because Dad had had to attend an unexpected conference about textiles and couldn't get away. They had waited, but the next weekend had been just as busy for Dad, so, in the end, Mrs. Turner had driven the car, with Ken spelling her in stretches.

The rhythmic slip-slap of the waves against the rocky shore was a familiar, well-loved sound. So were the noises on the roof—sap, catkins, acorns, pine cones falling with sudden loud plops—or the rapid patter of scampering squirrels and chipmunks. The breeze that fluttered the covers and blew across Kit's face carried the remembered spice of pine and hemlock.

The salmon sky above the hills, framed by her east window, the twittering and chirping of the birds that nested under the eaves, and the warmth of the sun on her face told her that it was very early. The shaft of sunlight, falling between two towering pines, slanted across her bed only in the very early morning, and the birds would settle down to quiet later on.

"Fee-bee—fee-bee," a bird shrilled and Kit smiled, remembering her mother's annual battles with the phoebe bird, determined to nest on the house.

She stretched full-length, wiggling her toes under the blankets. It was wonderful to be back at Lake Champlain. School was behind her. Two and a half lazy months in this beloved spot lay ahead.

She rolled over on her stomach, hugging the pillow under her face with both arms. She didn't need to open her eyes to see the room she loved. It was unsealed and the years had given the wood a warm satin patina. The walls rose about seven feet and above that it was open to the shadowy rafters and peaks of the roof.

Two dormers opened out into the trees on the lake side, offering glimpses of lawn sloping down to the flat gray rocks of the shore and the ever-changing expanse of water, bounded by the steep primeval hills of the opposite shore, still unmarred by summer cottages and other signs of human habitation.

Light green sailcloth draperies hung at the windows and curtained off one corner of the room to make a closet for Kit's clothes. Among the sweaters and skirts, the shorts and shirts behind those sailcloth curtains hung the aqua party dress. The thought of it made Kit writhe.

She propped herself on her elbow to look out the window. There was no wind and the lake was a length of silvery

satin, tinged with pink in the east, stretched taut between
the green shores. She would like to be out on it now, but she
knew the rowboats and her canoe would not have been put
in the water yet. Only the *Kittyken,* which had been returned yesterday from storage, would be riding gracefully at
anchor in the ell of the dock which ran out from the flat
rocks.

The *Kittyken* was a thirty-five-foot craft Dad had bought
last year. Mrs. Turner, laughing and looking very pretty, her
white dress and big white earrings bringing out her deep
smooth tan, had broken a bottle over her prow and christened her the *Kittyken,* for Kit and Kenneth. Ken was permitted to run all over the lake in her, just as he could drive
the car into town or anywhere else now that he had a license, but Kit wasn't allowed to take the boat out alone or
even to back the car into the old barn. Everyone treated Ken
as a grownup. Except for thrusting her into this business of
boys and dates and poise at parties, no one seemed to remember that, after all, Kit was nearly fifteen—well, fourteen, anyway. Funny how parents expected you to be grownup in all
the ways you didn't especially care about, but persisted in
regarding you as a child in any of the ways that really mattered to you.

No sense lying here grousing about all that was wrong
with her summer. That was no way to start a vacation. It
was quite evident she wasn't going back to sleep again. With
Marge and Babs gallivanting around other countries, she
would have to get used to doing things by herself. Maybe
she couldn't go out in a boat at the moment, but there was
nothing to stop her from having a swim before breakfast.

She swung her feet out of bed. As she did so, she knocked

off the stuffed honey-colored cocker spaniel that had been sharing the bed with her. She stooped quickly to pick up the toy.

"Sorry, Taffy, old boy, I didn't know you were so near the edge," she said, patting him gently as she placed him tenderly on the pillow.

Taffy was life-size and so amazingly real that there was no way to tell him from a flesh-and-blood cocker, except that he did not breathe. Mrs. Turner had given him to Kit a couple of years ago. He had been an expensive gift and Kit understood that he had been bought with "Mother's money." Mrs. Turner had a small income of her own which her husband would not permit her to spend on ordinary family or household expenses. Father said he was a Yankee, and that meant thrift— "Eat it up, wear it out, make it do, do without." He would support his family himself, but Mother, with lavish Southern extravagance, could provide the frills if she chose. So luxurious extras usually were bought with "Mother's money."

Mrs. Turner had vetoed Kit's request for a real dog because she felt that a city apartment was no place for one, and she knew from experience that after the first novelty had worn off the care of the pet would fall to her. Hoping to soften Kit's disappointment, she had bought Taffy, but although he was very handsome he could not take the place of a live dog so far as Kit was concerned.

"Though I'd rather have Taffy," Kit said now, "than that silly excuse for a dog Elaine gushes over."

Her bags were not yet unpacked, but she rummaged around in the chest under the window until she found a swim suit from last summer. It was streaked and faded and had long since lost its elasticity, so that it hung in unbecoming baggy fullness. But what difference did that make? There would be no one to see her this early in the morning.

She put it on quickly, tied her heavy rust-colored hair up on top of her head with a ribbon, and went carefully and quietly down the hall. She didn't have to worry about waking Ken—it took a good deal to do that—but she didn't want to disturb Aunt Charlotte in the west room.

It was hard to move noiselessly in the old house, the first summer cottage to be built along this strip of the Vermont shore opposite the Palisades. Kit's great-grandfather, a Vergennes merchant, had built it for his family many years ago. It was a long rectangle of a house with dormers and a peaked roof. A wide verandah ran all sixty feet on the lake side and a small sheltered porch faced over the meadows to the Green Mountains in back. Sturdy and strong, it had stood the winds and storms, the snow and ice of this lake country for nearly seventy years.

Changes had been made over the years. Electricity and an automatic pump now took the place of the kerosene lamps and hand-pumped water of Dick Turner's boyhood. An electric refrigerator replaced the huge blocks of ice cut in winter from the lake. The old wood-burner that had given out such warmth and cheer had made way for a shiny white gas stove. Last year, as one wall of the living room, Dad had put in a picture window which framed trees and lake and opposite hills.

Kit felt her way cautiously down the narrow, dark, closed-in stairway, crossed the big living room with its breath-taking window and huge fireplace, and let herself out the front

The stone steps leading down to the lake were cold to her bare feet and slippery with pine needles. She drew a deep breath. It smelled so good—clean, fresh, and aromatic. She loved it, she loved this spot, and not Aunt Charlotte, nor Elaine, nor the aqua formal and all it entailed—nothing was going to spoil her summer.

4

"Bird-Song at Morning"

At the bend in the gray stone stairs, Kit stopped in surprise. The *Kittyken,* gleaming mahogany and brass, was not riding alone in the ell of the dock, as she had expected. On one side of the big boat were the two canoes—Ken's and hers—and on the other, the skiff and the flat-bottomed rowboat. Evidently George, the man who opened and closed the cottage each year, had put them in. He must have known how impatient she would be to get out on the lake. Of course she and Ken would have to haul out the boats and canoes to calk and paint them, but it was wonderful to have them in the water now.

She could paddle down to the river and save her swim for her return. She put on the wrinkled terry-cloth bathing coat that was now too short and too tight, and tied it firmly around her waist. It took only a moment to get the paddles from the pump house. Then she was untying the painter and stepping lightly down into her canoe.

She had the world to herself at this early hour. There were no boats on the lake and the rocky shores were quiet and deserted. The ice-blue crepe satin surface of the lake rippled away from her canoe and when she lifted her paddle, the drops fell back in showers of jewels.

Beyond the spit of land that ran out into the lake, forming the big bay at the mouth of the river, she could see the soft blue outline of Camel's Hump in the Green Mountains. *Lion Couchant,* Sleeping Lion, the French-Canadians called it, but Kit thought it looked more like the profile of a giant Indian lying on his back with the hump as his nose.

There was no color, she thought for the hundredth time, that was more gorgeous than the hue of the Green Mountains, seen from Lake Champlain. On her left Diamond Island stood out clearly, divided into two islets now with the lake so high. Its feathery trees, so much like palms in distant outline, and the white streak of its beach, gave it the exotic look of a tropical isle, dropped down incongruously into New England's Lake Champlain.

She was paddling past the Gunnersons' now. The smooth green lawns rose steeply to the big, verandah-encircled house. Looking up at the length of it, crowning the top of the slope, she thought again how appropriate was the Indian name, *Thendara,* meaning Long House. The dark trunks of the straight, tall pines, from which the lower branches had been cut away, were black lines in a rhythmic pattern of light and dark against the pale blue sky.

There was no sign of life about the place. Kit felt a twinge of loneliness coupled with resentment that strangers should be summering in Marge's house. She wondered if the new tenants had arrived and what they were like. Beyond the Gunnersons' was the little cove with the sandy beach where she, Babs, Marge and Ken had learned to swim.

On the other side of the cove the shore was lower, sloping

gently back almost level with the lake. There were cottages here, smaller and closer together, all along the shore up to the arm of land that formed the bay.

This little peninsula belonged to the Summers. The long retaining wall gleamed white, and above it Kit could see gay parasols. Under the boathouse the Summers' speedboat bobbed gently.

Between Split Rock and Thompson's Point, Sloop Island loomed for all the world like a ship in the distance. Seeing it like this in the early morning light, Kit could understand how, in Revolutionary days, the British Commander Carleton had mistaken it for a ship and fired on it.

It was a long pull across the wide bay. Kit rounded the point and slipped quietly into the river. It was so lovely, so still, she hardly dared breathe. The canoe glided smoothly through beds of slippery lily pads that would be dotted with a glory of yellow, pink and white a little later. There was a flash of crimson over her head as two red-winged blackbirds skimmed across the river. A huge turtle sunning itself on a fallen log, was reflected clearly on the polished surface of the water.

"My, you're a big fellow," Kit called to him. "You'd make wonderful soup." Her voice sounded high and clear in the quiet of the early morning.

What was that floating toward her on the current? Could it be a water snake? And then she saw that it was an oar, a bright new oar, its varnish gleaming as it bobbed along. She turned the canoe toward it and when it was near enough, reached out and pulled it in. Where had it come from? There were no houses down here near the mouth of the river and no boat anywhere in sight.

Of course, Kit couldn't see very far up the river. She was sure the Otter was the twistingest, turningest river in the world. There were some twenty-eight bends in the short distance to Vergennes—about eight miles by car. And the turns were so sharp that each one seemed the end until one was right on top of it.

Well, she would paddle around the next bend or so and see if there was anyone stupid enough to lose an oar. She headed straight for the wooded shore that seemed to form a complete circle making the river a little lake. When she drew near, she could see the outlet where the river curved to the left. As she rounded the turn she saw the boat, a slim gray skiff riding at anchor in the middle of the river. A young man, his long-visored cap tipped forward to keep the slanting rays of the early-morning sun out of his eyes, reclined indolently against the backrest of the middle seat, his arms folded back of his head.

Sure enough an oar trailed from one oarlock, the other was empty.

"Hi, there," Kit called. "Did you lose an oar?"

The young man took off his cap and waved it in salute. "Yes," he shouted back. "Did you meet it somewhere?" As the canoe drew alongside the boat, he went on, "It slipped out of the oarlock a while back and went floating away on a journey of its own. I've been resting here, waiting for some Good Samaritan to bring it back."

Kit was stunned. She stared at him as if he were some strange species she had never encountered before.

"You mean you just let the oar slip out and float away," she asked incredulously, "and didn't even try to get it back?"

He shrugged. "There didn't seem to be much I could do

about it except sit tight and trust that some kind soul would
return it."

"But it's so early, you couldn't expect anyone to be around.
It might have drifted across the lake or down to Ticonderoga. Would you just have sat here all day?"

"I could do worse," he said, laughing. "When I nosed
around that bend, it was so hushed and quiet I felt I'd in-
truded on the Garden of Eden. The water was pink with
the sunrise and so clear and still everything 'floated double'
like Wordsworth's Swan, and I couldn't tell reality from re-
flection."

His voice was deep and full and musical. Kit was thrilled
in spite of herself. He enunciated with a fastidiousness she
found unusual, accustomed as she was to the sloppy speech
of the average high-school boy. And no high-school boy she
knew would dream of quoting poetry in this matter-of-fact,
unabashed way.

"The willows along the shore were pale-green curtains,
waving softly in the ghost of a breeze," he went on, apparently encouraged by Kit's rapt expression. "I got to repeating 'The Lady of Shalott'—you know, 'By the margin, wil-
low-veiled . . .' After a time I heard birds singing, and I
was quoting Stevenson:

I will make you brooches and toys for your delight
Of bird-song at morning and star-shine at night.

Kit listened, enthralled. Though he was slouched down in
the boat, she could tell from the length of his legs that he
must be very tall. She had never seen a thinner boy. The
bones of his face stood out sharply. His deep-set eyes were

brilliant blue, shadowed by long, thick lashes. His hair which
had not been sheered by a crew cut, was black and tousled a
little now by what he had called the "ghost of a breeze."

*And you shall wash your linen and keep your body white
In rainfall at morning and dewfall at night.*

He was continuing in that low, rich voice that sent tingles
over Kit. "That was when the kingfisher skimmed past, and
I swung around and knocked the oar overboard. Clumsy,
wasn't I?"

Kit giggled. She suddenly realized that the giggle sounded
for all the world like the noises made by those silly girls at
school who so disgusted her.

"A bit careless, certainly." The beauty of his voice and the
charm of his smile seemed to be weaving some sort of spell.
A strange excitement quickened her breath and made her
throat tight.

"Who would be careful on a day like this?" he answered.
"It's part of the beauty of the morning to be rescued by a
lovely maid with flaming hair."

Kit sat there in tongue-tied confusion, furious with herself
for blushing. It had never mattered to her how she looked
when any of the boys in the crowd or any of Ken's friends
were around. But now she was suddenly conscious of her
worn, tight coat and her faded, baggy bathing suit.

"I am glad I found your oar," she said stiffly. She picked
up her paddle and pushed out of the shade of the willows.
"I must get back for breakfast."

"Thanks for the oar and for the perfect touch to the
beauty of the morning," he said, and called after her,

Gorgeous she entered the sunlight
Which gathered her up in a flame.

The full, deep tones hung over the water. Kit paddled on in a daze. Suddenly a strange new dreamlike quality had been added to the radiance of the morning. Was this the sort of thing that had happened to those other girls, the thing she had never understood?

Why, oh why, had she gone out in these faded, last year's clothes? What a simpleton he must have thought her, simpering and blushing at his teasing compliments, and all the time looking such a mess.

As she paddled slowly back along the shore, she wondered who he was, where he came from, and if she would see him again.

When she drew near her own dock, she saw Ken standing on the ell waving and shouting.

"For Pete's sake," he called. "Where've you been?"

"Down the river," she answered. "Why? What's the matter?"

"Good grief, do you know what time it is? Breakfast's been ready for hours. Mother and Aunt Charlotte are having a fit."

She tossed him the line of her canoe and he made it fast, while she stepped up on the dock, threw off her coat, ran out to the deep end and dived cleanly into the water with hardly a splash. She tingled all over at the shock of the cold water, and she swam fast with a graceful coordination of her movements that made her a joy to watch.

"Come on," Ken growled. "Breakfast's waiting and I'm starved." He was big like his father, but he had his mother's dark eyes and hair. In a week, Kit thought enviously, he would be a smooth, even bronze. She pulled herself up the steps of the ladder and ran lightly up the dock in a spray of glittering drops.

Her mother and Aunt Charlotte were waiting on the porch. Kit was uncomfortably conscious that Aunt Charlotte's glance lingered on her old, ill-fitting suit.

"Katharine!" Sally Turner used her daughter's given name only when annoyed. "How inconsiderate of you to go off like this without leaving any word for us, keeping us all waiting for breakfast. We'll go ahead now. Hurry and join us."

Kit sped up the dark narrow stairs. All the time she was dressing, and brushing her damp hair, a pair of deep-set, very blue eyes smiled at her, and she could hear a deep voice saying, "I will make you brooches and toys for your delight . . ."

She stopped with the brush in her upraised hand and studied herself earnestly in the mirror. Although her eyes looked unusually bright, her brows and lashes were the same silly pale gold and her uptilted nose was already powdered with freckles. She sighed.

5

No, No, Mrs. Phoebe!

Floating in a trancelike state of dreamy unreality, Kit took a long time to dig out a shirt and shorts from her suitcase and put them on. The others had finished breakfast when she came downstairs.

Aunt Charlotte said with heavy humor, "The late Miss Turner at last!" and regarded the shirt and shorts with distaste. Kit had overheard her telling Mother that she could not understand how girls could bear to go around dressed eternally in pants—it was so unfeminine.

"Martha is keeping your breakfast warm in the kitchen," Mrs. Turner told Kit coldly, "but you'll have to wash up your dishes. She has too much to do to serve two breakfasts."

Aunt Charlotte's evident disapproval and her mother's cold annoyance made no impression on Kit. She smiled sweetly and vaguely, and went into the kitchen. "Bird-song at morning . . ." She must look up that poem. She had never heard it before, and though the boy in the boat had mentioned the author, she couldn't remember the name. Maybe the librarian in Vergennes could help her.

When she saw the broad back of the woman washing dishes at the sink, she bounced back to reality and squealing, "Martha," she rushed to embrace her.

Martha turned, her pretty face beaming. "Ki-it," she exclaimed in a singing drawl that made two syllables of it. "I've been lookin' for you, lamb. How are you?"

"Fine," Kit gave her a resounding kiss, thinking as she had a hundred times how little Martha resembled the spare, taciturn Vermonters she read about in books. Martha was almost as broad as she was tall, and her ample curves gave her a soft, comfortable look. Her round face with its sparkling blue eyes was framed in short curly black hair. She loved to talk in her soft, singing drawl, and her laughter was quick and hearty.

"How are you?" Kit said. "And how was the winter here?" Martha's face sobered. "It was a hard winter, Kit," she answered, shaking her head. "I ain't seen so much snow and ice in years. The big wool mill near Burlington closed down and moved south, you know, and that left a lot of men out of work. Seems Vermont's gettin' to have only two industries—dairyin' and summer people. Last winter the fishin' villages on the ice were bigger'n ever." She was pouring milk and dishing up scrambled eggs as she talked.

Kit sat down at the little table by the window and began to drink her orange juice. "I've often thought how funny it must look to see those fishing shacks scattered all over the lake," she said.

Though she had never seen Champlain in winter, she had often come upon the weathered gray fishing shacks stored here and there in the woods along the shore. They were no bigger than good-sized closets, with holes in the floors through which the fishermen dropped the exceedingly long lines they used for the Lake Champlain smelts, which were a delicacy on hotel menus and commanded a special price in city markets.

"They ain't scattered all over the lake exactly," Martha said. "They're usually grouped together. Fishville in Burlington Harbor had over a hundred shacks last winter with a duly elected mayor and all." She emptied her dishpan and began to dry the dishes.

"It can be a dangerous business, and last winter was mighty bad. Some-a the time early in the winter they were fishin' on only four or five inches of ice. When a north blow sets in, the ice floes move around, and anythin's liable to happen. You remember the Howards who lived down the river road. Will Howard lost his job when the mill moved south. Since then he's been fishin', sellin' bait, anything to earn a few pennies. He was fishin' one night in a north wind when a piece broke off a big floe and went a-sailin' down the lake with three shanties on it. The Coast Guard took off to rescue the men, but afore they got 'em, Will Howard was drowned, though he had managed to save young Clay Foster, who was fishin' with him."

Kit put down her glass. "Martha, how dreadful! Wasn't he the man with all the children who used to sell bait on the river road?"

"Yep, that was him," Martha nodded. "Fishville took up a collection, and the veterans held a benefit for Molly, but what they got don't go very far with seven young ones to feed and clothe."

Martha's story of the Howard tragedy took away Kit's appetite, and she began to stack her dishes.

"Molly took the younger children over to her cousin Trudy Clark's in Bristol, and the older boys are with her aunt in Panton. But they can't stay long at the Clarks'. They have three children of their own, and Trudy is expecting another. Anyways, there's no work for Molly in Bristol. Nothing much over there but lumberin' and lumber products. If Molly could only get back to Vergennes, maybe she could get a job in Fisher's department store or something." Busily cutting shortening into flour for a pie, she went on. "There's a little house for sale on the road out toward the poor farm, but for all its tumble-down condition, Steve White wants two thousand for it, and that's about all Molly has in the world."

Kit had collected her dishes and was running water into the dishpan when Martha sang out, "Someone's a-comin'."

Kit crossed to the window. A small, tawny dog with a creamy plume of tail arched over his back was running down the driveway ahead of a blond girl in a yellow dress.

"It's Elaine Lester," Kit told Martha. "You remember the Lesters who used to spend a week or so with us now and then?"

"You bet."

"They've rented the Wheaton cottage for the summer."

"You don't say. I heard the place was rented."

Bowl in hand, Martha came over to stand beside Kit. "My, she's pretty as a picture, ain't she? Looks kinda like a doll."

Coming down the driveway under the sixty-foot pines, Elaine seemed especially small and fragile. Her pale gold hair danced in bouncing little curls over her small head. In just the one short week that she had been at the lake, her creamy skin had taken on a golden tone. She was carrying something with great care, stepping cautiously along the uneven driveway. She waved as she saw Kit standing at the window.

"Hi," she called. "How was your trip?"

"Not bad," Kit let her in the back door, the usual entrance for visitors at lakeside cottages. "Mother and Aunt Charlotte are on the porch. Shall we go out?"

Elaine nodded. "I baked this cake for your mother, and I have a message for her from my mother."

Mrs. Turner and Aunt Charlotte were steadying a chair on which Ken was standing, as he tried to dislodge the nest the phoebe bird had built on the porch light.

"You *aren't* going to make him take it down when there are eggs in it, Sally Belle," Aunt Charlotte was protesting.

"I certainly am," Mrs. Turner's tone was determined. "Mrs. Phoebe is a very careless housekeeper, and I'm not going to give her a chance to shower my house, my guests, and my family with her old mites."

"What's the use, Mother?" Ken said. "If I know Mrs. Phoebe, she'll only build another nest somewhere else on the house by tomorrow."

This was an annual battle. As soon as Mrs. Phoebe had been dislodged from one nest, she built another—on the porch or over the back door. She must share the house with the Turners. As determined as a phoebe bird, Kit thought, would mean the acme of dogged resolution.

Ken stepped down from the chair, gingerly holding the nest at arm's length, and saw the girl in the doorway.

"Hi, Elaine," he called. "Swell to have you at the lake for the whole summer."

"It's wonderful to be here," Elaine said, "but it has been lonely." She looked up at Kenneth with her blue eyes wide. "I'm glad the Turners have arrived at last."

Kit thought, she might just as well have said she's glad *he's* here at last. Watch him puff up.

Elaine greeted Aunt Charlotte and presented her cake to Mrs. Turner. "I made it this morning—from scratch, too," she said with pardonable pride. "No mixes for me."

It looked like an advertisement for one of her despised mixes, Kit thought—round and high and covered thickly with soft, creamy coconut frosting.

Everyone oh'd and ah'd in admiration. Elaine's little dog, Ah-Ting, made them laugh by sitting up on his hind legs and begging in front of Mrs. Turner, who was holding the cake.

"Isn't he precious?" Elaine squealed. She cuddled him up in her arms, cooing, "Toe tweet, toe loving, him's a precious." It made a pretty scene, the blond girl in the yellow dress and the silky, tawny little dog. Kit was sure Elaine realized it full well.

"Your cake is a picture," Aunt Charlotte gave Elaine an approving pat. "Congratulations. A girl who is interested in womanly accomplishments is rare these days."

"And how!" Ken agreed feelingly. "That's one of the reasons I'm trying to stake a claim to this golden armful before these lakeside wolves get wise."

Elaine giggled. "I'll bake you a cherry pie, Kenny boy," she said easily, "but you know I'm a young thing and cannot leave my mother."

Kit, remembering her own tongue-tied awkwardness earlier that morning, sighed enviously.

Elaine turned to Mrs. Turner. "Mother wants to know what you people are doing about the Fourth of July dance at the club tonight. Also, she's driving to town in about an hour, and she wondered if anyone would like to go with her."

"Thank your mother for me," Mrs. Turner said. "But, much as I hate it, I'm afraid I must unpack. How about you, Aunt Charlotte?"

Aunt Charlotte, still beaming delightedly on Elaine, said that she, too, must unpack. "But I'd be grateful if your mother would buy me a hair net. I tore mine last night, and in the wild winds of Champlain I need one."

"Tell your mother we'll all be looking in on the dance for a while," Mrs. Turner said. "Suppose we stop for you about nine."

"I'll take care of Elaine myself," Ken put in quickly. "How about it, Elaine? Is it a date? I'll pick you up in the *Kittyken.*"

"That will be just wonderful," Elaine gushed, giving Ken a full treatment of starry-eyed smiles. Kit wondered if she hadn't baked the cake with exactly this in mind.

"Stick around a minute, will you?" Ken was still holding the bird's nest at arm's length. "I have to get rid of this, but I'll be right back."

When he returned, he told them: "I met the people who have the Gunnerson place for the summer. There's a son a little older than I am. He seems a right guy. He said he'd heard the kids around here played tennis mornings on the Gunnerson courts and he'd be happy to have us continue to use them. Glad to have us any time. What do you say we take the *Kittyken* and round up some of the gang for to-morrow morning."

"Swell," Kit's enthusiasm held a note of relief. "I've been wondering what we'd do this year about tennis."

"I'll have to tell Mother she has no passengers for town," Elaine said.

"I'll run you over in the *Kittyken*," Ken offered.

"Thanks," Elaine said and added, smiling up at Ken. "Poor little old me wouldn't dare play tennis with an expert like you, Ken."

As if he were Bill Tilden himself, and the big boob swallows it and beams, Kit thought in disgust.

"But I'd just love to sit on the sidelines and watch you," Elaine finished.

No eyes for anyone else of course, Kit thought, and then she laughed. If she didn't watch out she'd get to be a dis-agreeable old sourpuss without a kind word for anybody. She should be cheering. It was grand to know there would be tennis this year, even though the Gunnersons were not here. This reassurance almost made up for the unhappy thought of the dance tonight. She knew from her mother's attitude that it would be useless to try to get out of it. But while she sat with her mother and Aunt Charlotte, embar-rassed, bored and utterly miserable, she could sustain herself with the thought that tomorrow there would be tennis as usual.

6

A Dance Is Not a Ping-Pong Party

"Your yellow cotton will do for tonight," her mother said when Kit went up to dress. "Save the aqua for a special party. But wear your good patent leather pumps. I just can't take those ballet shoes with which your generation delights in ruining its feet."

Kit went on upstairs with the air of a martyr about to be thrown to the lions. It was when she was in the shower repeating to the splash of the water, "I will make you brooches and toys for your delight . . . ," that the thought suddenly dazzled her, with the brilliance of a Fourth of July skyrocket, that she might see the boy in the boat at the club.

The club was a small one to which most of the summer families up and down the lakeshore belonged. There was a protected little harbor for motorboats and sailboats, with rafts and diving platforms for swimming. The house itself was low and square with a wide veranda overlooking the lake. There was a game room for pool, billiards, and ping-pong, as well as a small card room, a dining room, and a big ballroom for dances and parties.

The dances, like this Fourth of July party, were well attended. If the boy in the boat were staying with anyone on this part of the Vermont shore, it was very likely he would be at the club tonight.

The idea of seeing him again filled Kit with excitement. She began to take extraordinary pains with her appearance. She brushed her hair until her arms ached and pushed it carefully into gleaming wide, deep waves. She had to remove her lipstick with tissue and put it on all over again before it suited her. She toyed with the idea of wearing the aqua dress, but she knew it was too dressy for the first party of the summer. Besides her mother would certainly think it strange if, right away and on her own initiative, she wore the dress to which she had objected so strongly.

She wished she had some mascara to darken her sandy brows and lashes, but she had never owned any, and her mother had no need to use it. Kit had never bothered with make-up, using even lipstick only on special occasions when she remembered it. She thought fleetingly of trying to darken her brows with a lead pencil, but she was afraid it might not look quite right.

She did borrow her mother's expensive perfume and used it so lavishly that Mrs. Turner exclaimed when at last Kit came downstairs, "Heavens, Kit, you positively reek. I don't mind your using my perfume for the proper occasion, but use it with discretion. Perfume is a good deal stronger than toilet water, you know, and a drop or two is plenty."

All the way to the club, sitting between Aunt Charlotte and her mother, Kit kept hoping the boy in the boat would be at the party. Above Aunt Charlotte's white head through the side window she saw a star. It wasn't the evening star, but she wished on it just the same—wished he would be there and would ask her to dance. At the thought of his arms around her and his intense blue eyes smiling into hers, her heart began to beat in a strange breathless rhythm.

The club veranda was gay with enormous silk lanterns donated by Mr. Gunnerson, who had brought them from China. Kit followed her mother and Aunt Charlotte into the big room with a wide fireplace at the far end and long windows opening on the porch on the lake side. Already she felt shy and awkward, and butterflies fluttered in her stomach. She was behaving ridiculously, she told herself. This was only an informal gathering of friends and neighbors. No one would be particularly interested in her, in how she looked, or in what she did. But she couldn't help realizing with another part of her mind that Aunt Charlotte, her mother, and those same friendly neighbors *would* notice if she were tongue-tied and ill at ease, and if no one asked her to dance.

For a few moments there was the bustle and confusion of greeting. Her mother was speaking to friends she had not seen since last summer and introducing Aunt Charlotte to those she did not know. Aunt Charlotte was smiling and gracious. Mr. Stiles and Walker Higgins hurried over to pay her extravagant compliments. Aunt Charlotte laughed and talked with them, quite aware that even at seventy she was feminine and charming.

Kit felt childish and stupid, trailing in their wake. If only someone had asked to take her to this party, as Ken had Elaine. To arrive later with an escort, cherished and cared for, might not be so bad. If only the boy in the boat would appear and claim her.

The evening dragged along, but no blue-eyed, black-

haired, poetry-quoting boy put in an appearance. Elaine arrived with Ken, laughing and throwing off the spangled
scarf with which she had guarded her curls in the *Kittyken*.
She was wearing a pale pink nylon dress with a full skirt
over many crinolines and looked as sweet and tempting as a
bon-bon.

All the boys—and the men, too—clustered around her.
She giggled and coquetted, having a wonderful time. When
the dancing began, she and Ken hardly made the circuit of
the room before someone cut in. From then on, Ken had to
be on his toes to manage any time with her at all.

After a while Kit wandered into the game room. A couple
of twelve-year-olds were playing ping-pong, and three or four
older boys were shooting billiards. Kit was watching the
ping-pong players when a small girl with a bobbing black
pony tail joined her. Kit recognized her as Ray Tabor's sister
Cheryl.

"Come on, Cherry, have a game," the boys invited.

"Okay," Cherry answered amiably. "But let's make it
doubles." She turned to Kit. "Aren't you Ken Turner's
sister?"

There it was again for the trillionth time, Kit thought
wryly, as she smiled and nodded at Cheryl. Didn't anyone
recognize her for herself? Would she always exist only in the
shadow of her popular brother?

"Ray says you're a whiz at ping-pong," Cheryl said. "He
says you're a natural like Babe Didrikson Zaharias was and
that you can beat any of them—the boys, too, I mean—at
most any sport."

"I'm not quite that good," Kit said, laughing, "but I think
all sports are fun."

"Would you—will you play a game of ping-pong with us?" Cheryl asked diffidently.

Kit, amused that Cheryl should be shy with her, evidently regarding her as that magic creature, an older girl, smilingly agreed. She would play her best, she decided, because she did not believe in presenting even children with false victories they had not won. However, the youngsters were good enough to make it interesting for her. Cheryl's serve had a slice that made it very effective, and her partner was so quick he could handle Kit's swift returns.

Ping-pong is a fast game and after a couple of sets Kit was subconsciously aware that she was no longer the carefully turned out young lady in impeccable party attire of a few short hours ago. Successfully accomplishing an almost impossible return, she had ripped the right sleeve from the armhole of her yellow dress; her face was flushed and shiny; her carefully arranged hair blown every which way. Kit did not care; she was enjoying herself for the first time that evening.

Her swift and devastating play attracted the attention of the boys at the billiard table and before long, the ping-pong players had a laughing, cheering gallery.

Cheryl's brother Ray rooted for Kit, whom he had known for years as Ken's little sister. He was stocky and not much taller than Kit, but he was quick and sure on his feet as a cat. His crew cut was dark and bristling, and his black eyes were full of laughter.

"Go to it, Brick Top," he encouraged on the difficult plays and, "atta girl, Brick Top," he applauded the successful ones.

Soon an impromptu elimination doubles tournament was organized. Kit found herself playing with Ray Tabor. He was a fast player and they made a good team. He was fun too, with his jokes and nonsense. Kit hadn't laughed so much in a long time.

One by one the other teams went down to defeat before the Turner-Tabor combination. The victors, Ray and Kit, were breathing hard. Kit was sure she must be completely disheveled, but she was having too much fun to bother about her appearance. In reality, she looked glowing and alive and very attractive. Her bright hair clung in damp curls around her flushed face. Her blue eyes were brilliant with excitement.

"You've grown up to be quite a gal, Brick Top," Ray told her. "My type exactly, and a swell partner. This has mincing around a silly ballroom beat a mile. Let's you and me take on the waterfront this summer."

"I'm willing," Kit said, laughing, "but watch out the waterfront doesn't take us over instead."

"Katharine," said her mother's voice behind her, "I've been looking for you everywhere. Aunt Charlotte and I are ready to leave."

Embarrassed, Kit said good night quickly and followed her mother. Like a small child being taken home to bed by its mother, she thought in hot, shamed misery. Mother's so anxious for me to grow up and be a lady. How does she think I feel when she treats me like a baby in public?

Aunt Charlotte was waiting at the back door. "We haven't seen you all evening, Katharine," she said. "Where in the world have you been?"

"In the game room," Kit answered shortly, and her mother added in a voice of exasperation, "Evidently Kit spent the entire evening playing ping-pong!"

Aunt Charlotte surveyed her niece with ill-concealed disfavor, "Still a tomboy, Katharine, I see."

As if the world held no lower form of life, Kit told herself. It probably doesn't to Aunt Charlotte, who thinks girls should sit on a fine cushion and sew a fine seam—or bake a picture cake and flutter their eyelashes at the young men.

Later in the car, her mother said in a tone of resignation, "Really, Kit, why can't you behave like other girls? You know very well a dancing party is not the time or place for a young lady to play ping-pong all evening."

Aunt Charlotte added in a purring voice, "Wasn't Elaine adorable? There's no doubt that *she* was the belle of the ball."

Kit set her teeth. Grownups make me sick—sick, sick, sick—she thought in impotent fury. Then, like a talisman, the words, "I will make you brooches and toys for your delight . . ." echoed in her mind. She heard the deep voice, saw a smile in shadowed blue eyes, and was lost in a dream again. Her ignominious departure, Aunt Charlotte, her mother, Ray Tabor—none of them mattered.

7

That Boy in the Boat

The long driveway snaked a blue-stone swath between the green lawns, tennis courts and gardens of Thendara. Everything looked as usual. Kit could hardly believe that roly-poly Marge with her ready laughter and amusing nonsense would not run out to greet them. But when they circled in front of the long porch, there was a tall thin young man waiting at the foot of the steps. He came over to the car quickly, moving rapidly, though he was obviously lame.

He was smiling as he opened the car door. Kit, sitting with Elaine in the front seat, drew a quick, surprised breath. She was looking straight into the deep-set, dark-blue eyes of the young man in the boat.

"Welcome to Thendara," he said and added in her ear, as he helped her out of the car, "My good angel of the river. This *is* my lucky day."

Kit could feel herself blushing and was absolutely tongue-tied. If only she could have tossed back a gay reply! She stood awkwardly silent as Ken introduced her, Elaine, the Carey twins—Jane and Joan—Bud Summers, and Ray Tabor.

They stood in a group chatting while Ken parked the car. Their host was easy and friendly, and the crowd seemed to take to him at once. His name was Bates Cunningham. Kit thought it suited him—unusual and distinguished. Though he was past nineteen, he was entering Yale in the fall, when Ken and Ray would be freshmen at Dartmouth.

With just a hint of bitterness in his mellow voice, he spoke of his illness and explained that it had set him back a couple of years. No, it wasn't polio, but meningitis. It had nearly finished him—body and spirit—but he was more resigned to it now. Though it still was a nuisance to be lame, he could go on with the business of living, only occasionally beating his brains out in resentment at the things he couldn't do.

His lameness explained a lot, Kit thought. It was probably the reason he didn't know any better than to lose an oar. And no doubt he had read all that poetry while he was in the hospital with nothing more interesting to do. She found him beside her as they moved toward the tennis courts.

"A sort of pricking in my thumbs tells me you're a star at this," he said, indicating the tennis court. His mouth was smiling, but his eyes were serious. "Am I right?"

"What gives you that idea?"

"The way you move," he answered. "I noticed it yesterday morning. Just now I couldn't help thinking, 'she walks in beauty . . .' You would have to be good at sports."

Again Kit suffered the misery of not knowing how to answer, yet at the same time down underneath, waiting to be relished when she was alone, she was conscious of a wild singing gladness that he had chosen to walk with her and pay her compliments.

The courts were not in very good condition, but they decided to use the better one and agreed to put in some work on both of them in the early mornings.

"Hallelujah. I'm in luck!" Ray cried when he drew Kit as his partner. Bates winked at her knowingly.

She and Ray beat Joan and Ken six-four, and took on Jane and Bud. Kit almost caused them to lose the second set because her mind was not on the game. The non-players, Elaine and Bates, and those waiting for their turn to come up, since only one court was usable, had been sitting in a group on the grass under the trees, laughing and joking, applauding and occasionally ribbing the players. Halfway through the second set, Kit noticed that Ken and Joan were alone under the trees. She almost flubbed an easy lob. Where had Elaine and Bates gone off together?

Her playing became so erratic that finally Ray exclaimed in exasperation, "I'm your partner, Brick Top—remember? Quit this woolgathering and give me a little support, huh?"

Twice Ray had the score at set point only to have Kit lose the next point, but they finally managed to take the set eight-six.

Winded, Ray flung himself down on the grass. "We need practice all right, Brick Top," he said.

Kit was grateful for his use of the plural. He liked to win, and she supposed it was only because he thought she was good that he had been so pleased to have her for a partner. She was sorry she had almost let him down.

After a few minutes, the boys began a singles match, while the girls rested. Ray was giving a good account of himself against Ken.

Sitting on the grass between Joan and Jane, Kit watched the game in a sort of distracted way, while she kept an eye out for Bates and Elaine. Finally she saw them strolling across the lawn from the direction of the gardens. Bates was laughing down at Elaine, who was looking up at him and talking with animation.

For the rest of the morning, Kit laughed when the others did, answered when she had to, hoping she made sense. She could not erase from her mind the sight of Bates, his thin face alight with appreciation of Elaine's very feminine beauty and charm. What chance had Kit, shy, inexperienced, and not very pretty against a girl like Elaine?

This must be the way those silly girls had felt as they walked past Ken's door. She had laughed before; she could pity them now. If this was growing up, it was painful and she wanted no part of it. She'd rather be good old Kit, who asked nothing better than to pitch a swift ball. But because a thin, blue-eyed boy who had no better sense than to lose an oar had smiled at her, she knew she could never go back to that complacent, contented, good old Kit again.

The Turners had dinner in the middle of the day, country style, when Mr. Turner was in the city.

"Anybody want anything from town?" Mrs. Turner asked, while Martha was serving the dessert. "Aunt Charlotte and I are going up after dinner to do some marketing."

"I'd like to drive up with you," Kit said. "I want to go to the library."

Aunt Charlotte looked surprised. Mrs. Turner repeated in astonishment, "The library—why, Kit!" Ken let out a hoot. "Don't tell me you're planning to read a book—and on vacation, too! Take her temperature somebody, quick; she's delirious."

"What is so remarkable about my reading a book?" Kit asked crisply, nettled by the bombshell effect of her statement. "It wouldn't hurt you to read a book occasionally."

"Oh, I do," Ken answered amiably. "Occasionally—very occasionally."

"Martha says we need drinking water," Mrs. Turner told Ken. "Will you put the carboys in the car for me, please?"

Kit made a face at him, as they rose from the table. Ken put the bottles in the trunk compartment and wandered down to the *Kittyken*. The others, after collecting purses and shopping lists, went out to the car.

A soughing wind was blowing warm from the south. Looking down from the turn by the big pine tree, Kit could see great, slate-colored rollers pursuing each other up the lake. The distant Adirondacks were lost in haze. The blurred outline of the nearer ranges looked like a gray chiffon scarf tossed in haphazard folds against the pale sky. Heat shimmered across the meadows to the soft blue mass of the Green Mountains on the eastern horizon.

"City of Vergennes," announced the road sign proudly where they turned to cross the bridge over the falls. Once long ago, Vergennes had been a busy, bustling city. The falls of the Otter had furnished power for its grist and lumber mills. Here Macdonough had built the fleet that defeated the British in the battle of Plattsburg.

Now, despite the fact that its population was less than two thousand, Vergennes jealously guarded its city charter, elected its mayors, and was proud of being the smallest city in the United States.

Though Kit had never been a poetry lover, and this was

her first business visit to the library, she had committed to memory—as part of a store of lore gathered from her father about this beloved spot—a delightful poem about Vergennes by Arthur Guiterman, the poet who had made his home in Vermont, along with Dorothy Canfield, Robert Frost, Grandma Moses, Luigi Lucioni, Norman Rockwell, and a number of other writers and artists. Bates would love it, Kit thought. I'll say it for him the first chance I get.

The tree-shaded Main Street rose steeply from the bridge to the Inn which had been the old Stevens House, scene of brilliance and gaiety in days gone by. The long line of business establishments—filling stations, drugstores, restaurants, and a red-fronted A & P store—was broken here and there by lovely old houses. Beyond the Inn was the village green, a square of old velvety turf and great elms with a marble monument to Commodore Macdonough in the center, and on the right was the bandstand where the Thursday night concerts were held. Bordering the little park and extending along Main Street, big, comfortable homes of the vintage of bygone years spoke of gracious living. On the north side of the square was the large, two-story white house with its central doorway where her father had grown up. It belonged to a doctor now, and Kit had not been inside it for years.

"Let me out here, will you please?" she requested as, halfway up the hill, they passed the imposing Bixby Memorial Library. Built in 1912, it would have graced a city many times the size of Vergennes. At the head of the flight of stone steps, the tall columns of its portico rose to the full height of the square, two-storied buff building. A wide porch ran the full length of the left side, with a magnificent view over the valley to the distant Adirondacks. On clear days, Marcy, Saddleback, and eighteen other peaks were easily identifiable.

Inside, an imposing rotunda swept to the roof. On the left was a pleasant, sun-filled reading room, opening on the porch with its breathtaking view. On the right was the check out desk, and Kit saw, with a sinking feeling, that Mrs. Patterson Smith was in charge this afternoon.

"Bixby Memorial in Person," Kit said under her breath, for the austere Mrs. Smith's devotion to the library she directed was well known. She was a tall, thin woman with carefully dressed white hair. Her black eyes were sharp and direct, and her straight mouth was thin and firm.

She answered Kit's greeting perfunctorily, then turned back to look at her sharply. "Why, you're Dick Turner's daughter, aren't you?"

"Yes," Kit nodded. "I'm Katharine Turner." She wondered whether her father had used the library regularly when he was a boy and if Mrs. Smith had stamped his card when he borrowed books.

"You look like your father," Mrs. Smith said, "but evidently you are not the reader he was. You don't visit the library very often."

Kit admitted unhappily that she seldom borrowed books from the library, adding weakly that when she had time for such an inactive pursuit at the lake, she read some old books of her grandfather's she had found in the bookcases at the cottage.

Mrs. Smith was interested. Kit told her about an old history of Addison County with accounts of the settling and early history of Vergennes and neighboring towns.

"The author's name was Smith," Kit finished. "Was he a relative of yours?"

Mrs. Smith nodded. "My grandfather," she said. "It distressed him greatly that there was so little record of the early days, so he wrote . . . Will you excuse me just a minute?" she said, as a tall, brown-haired woman walked with a long, free stride from the reading room across the rotunda toward the door.

"Molly Howard, Molly Howard," Mrs. Smith called. "Wait a minute. I have a message for you."

Molly Howard—the widow of the man who had given his life to save his companion on the ice floe. Kit could not resist turning a little to look at her. There was a look of calm strength about Molly Howard. It was in her broad, square shoulders, her direct blue eyes, her large, firm mouth. Kit thought she would be a nice person to know—serene and brave, proud and independent.

Mrs. Smith talked with her for a moment or two and returned to Kit. "I am sorry to interrupt our talk," she apologized, "but I had an important message to give Mrs. Howard."

"I hope it was good news," Kit said impulsively. "I'm so sorry for her."

Mrs. Smith shook her head, her black eyes troubled. "I am afraid it wasn't," she said, and then, a little unwillingly, reluctant to discuss a friend's affairs, she added, "Mrs. Howard has been looking for a place to live in Vergennes. I had to tell her that one possibility—almost a last hope—is not available after all." She shook her head as if clearing it temporarily of Molly Howard's troubles and leaned toward Kit, "Is there something I can do for you?" she asked.

"I'm looking for a poem," Kit told her, feeling a little foolish. "I can't remember the author's name, but it goes something like this," and she quoted the lines about bird-song and star-shine that Bates had said to her.

Mrs. Smith smiled, but she looked puzzled. "It's lovely," she said, "but it's unfamiliar to me. I don't believe I ever heard it before. Come along while I consult Bartlett and some other authorities in the reading room."

Kit followed her into the quiet room with its west windows overlooking the valley to the distant Adirondacks, indistinct now in the haze.

As they entered the room, the young man sitting at a table in front of a huge fern, dripping green fronds from a six-foot stand, rose and came toward them. Kit recognized Bates Cunningham.

"Thanks so much," he said to Mrs. Smith. "I found exactly what I wanted."

"Hello there," he greeted Kit. "You're in good hands. Mrs. Smith knows where to find anything that has ever been printed."

"You flatter me." Mrs. Smith shook her head. "Katharine had just asked me about a poem I have never heard."

Oh, please, Kit thought desperately, *don't* tell him the poem. What will he think of me! "Never mind, Mrs. Smith," she interposed quickly. "It's all right. Some other time . . ." Inexorably Mrs. Smith repeated the lines, and Kit could feel her face burn with embarrassment.

"Ah," said Bates, cocking an eyebrow at Kit and adding to her confusion. "I'm the man who can help you with that. The poem is called 'Romance' and it's by Stevenson."

"Robert Louis?" Mrs. Smith asked in surprise. When Bates nodded, she continued, "We have his novels and essays, his *Child's Garden of Verses* in the children's room, but I'm sorry we have no other collection of his poems."

"I have the poem at home," Bates told her, "and I'll be glad to lend it to Kit."

"If you'll drive down with me," he said to Kit, "I'll get it for you now."

"I'll have to explain to my mother," Kit said, still uncomfortable over the situation in which Bates had caught her. "I came up with her. She's shopping somewhere in town."

"Wait till I put this book back," Bates said, "and we'll go and find her." They walked up Main Street and crossed over to the A & P. Lounging against its red front, a rangy old codger with a lined, tanned face under a battered hat eyed their shorts sardonically and croaked in disgust, "Summer's here."

Kit and Bates were laughing as they went into the store and found Mrs. Turner and Aunt Charlotte. Blushing, Kit presented Bates to them.

They stood for a moment exchanging small talk. Kit could see that the two ladies found Bates charming. When he told them that he was driving Kit back to the lake, Mrs. Turner looked pleased, and Aunt Charlotte, eying Kit's shirt and shorts disapprovingly, seemed surprised.

Bates's little car was a cream-colored Jaguar with red leather seats. In spite of her discomfiture, Kit stepped down into it with delight. She had always wanted to ride in a car like this. Wait until she told Ken! She felt very grown-up and sophisticated as the car swooped down the hill toward the bridge. The wind whipped her green scarf about her throat and blew her bright hair straight back from her face. She wished Babs and Marge could see her.

8

The Long Way Home

The cream-colored car swept across the bridge and turned into the road to the lake. Bates, busy with his driving, said nothing. The silence began to frighten Kit. In a panic, she tried desperately to think of something to say. As they passed the "City of Vergennes" road sign, she gave a feeble little laugh. "Vergennes is so proud of being a city," she said, indicating the marker.

"Some city," Bates said. "Fifteen hundred people and a couple of square blocks of houses and stores."

"But it *is* a city," Kit assured him earnestly, "with a mayor and everything. It's the smallest city in the United States and mighty proud of it."

"That's a curious thing to be proud about," Bates said. "What is there to be so set up about in that?"

He seemed very different today from the friendly, relaxed boy in the boat. Tense, frowning, he appeared to be at odds with everything.

Kit was a little taken aback. "Arthur Guiterman wrote a poem about it," she said defensively. "He understood the Vergennes spirit and admired it."

"When did a poet ever have any sense?" Bates said. "Well, O.K. What's the poem. Do you know?"

Kit almost wished she had held her tongue, but it was better, she decided, to argue with Bates than to ride all the way to the lake in silence.

"Can you recite it?" Bates asked a bit impatiently.

Kit replied in a voice she tried to keep steady, "The title is 'Vergennes, Vermont,' and it goes like this:

New York says, "I'm the finest in the nation,
With pretty near eight million population!"
Replies Vergennes (Vermont), "I do declare!
But I'm the smallest city anywhere!"
New York cries, "I'm the biggest, grandest, tallest!"
"You hear me?" says Vergennes, "I'm still the smallest."
Chicago thunders, "Since they founded Illion,
No town has grown like me with my three million!"
Vergennes brags, "Never, since the days of Priam,
Has any city been as small as I am!"
Detroit roars, "I've two million souls, I guess!"
Vergennes says, "I've a thousand, more or less."
Shouts Washington, "I'm larger every day;
How great I'll be this winter, who can say!"
Vergennes says, "I'm a fraction, I'm a decimal;
In fact, I claim to be infinitesimal."
Well, some like rocs or eagles, some like wrens;
Some love New York and some prefer Vergennes.

In spite of his moodiness, Bates laughed. "The poem's all right," he said. "But you can have Vergennes. Do you know where the name comes from?"

"It's French," Kit answered and blushed at the obviousness of her statement. "Back in the seventeen-eighties, the

French consul in New York, a man named Hector St. John Crèvecoeur, wrote to Ethan Allen and suggested that it would be a good idea if Vermont named her new towns after distinguished Frenchmen to show her gratitude for French help during the Revolutionary War."

"So, as I might have guessed, Vergennes is named for a Frenchman," Bates said with a shrug of indifference, "but you still haven't told me who he was."

"The Count de Vergennes the French minister of foreign affairs," Kit said quickly, "Crèvecoeur asked Allen to honor him by giving the name of Vergennes to the town to be laid out at the first falls of the Otter. And in 1786 the governor and council recommended the incorporation of the *City* of Vergennes."

They rode along for a few minutes in silence, then Bates said, "My father is a history professor. He'd probably be interested."

"If he's a history professor, he probably would," Kit said and gulped. Why in the world did she keep making such inane remarks?

"He teaches at Yale," Bates went on, "and writes historical novels that get on best-seller lists. Have you read *Dark Yesterday?*"

"No—no, I haven't," Kit admitted and rushed on in embarrassment, "your father certainly will be interested in this part of the country. A lot of history happened here."

"History happened here. Mind your alliteration, child," Bates mocked and then continued passionately, "history, history, history—I'm sick of the very word."

At Kit's startled, hurt expression, he reached over to pat her shoulder. "Don't mind me," he said apologetically. "I might be interested, too, if I weren't so dead set against majoring in history and following dutifully in my father's footsteps." After a long pause, he added, "But I suppose that's as good a deal as I could hope for."

Kit yearned to say something comforting, to assure him that he could have a wonderful life as a professor or in any other work he wanted to undertake; that his lameness made no difference, but the words would not come. The wind, blowing in gusts from the south, whipped her hair across her face. Nervously she pushed it back. "This wind will be tough for tennis, but it ought to make the skiing exciting," she said, and remembered too late that he could neither play tennis nor water-ski.

There was another uncomfortable pause, and then Bates turned to Kit with a smile, "What an idiot I am for inflicting my grouch on you. Forgive me, Kit, please."

His black hair was blown about by the wind, his thin cheeks were creased in a smile, his deep-set, startlingly blue eyes appealed for pardon. Kit's heart melted. "Silly," she said eagerly, "there's nothing to forgive."

"Then go on, tell me about this Vergennes at the first falls of the Otter. Who settled it to make a thriving city for your French consul and his count?"

Kit laughed. "All right," she said, feeling suddenly grown-up and confident. "You can make fun of it, if you like, but Vergennes once really was a thriving city. The falls gave power for its lumber and grist mills; there were ore beds and some manufacturing, and its merchants brought comforts to the settlers in the wilderness. And don't forget that it was here that Macdonough built the fleet that whipped the British!"

"Hear! Hear!" Bates applauded.

"It took slices of three towns—Panton, New Haven, and Ferrisburg—to make the city for my consul and his count," Kit went on, "Ferrisburg had been chartered to men from Dutchess County, New York; Panton and New Haven to men from Litchfield County, Connecticut. My father's people came from Connecticut."

"I can see how they came," Bates said, his good humor completely restored. "Up the lake and down the river to the falls."

"Sometimes in the very early morning when I'm alone on the water," Kit contributed happily, "I can almost see the canoes of the Indians gliding up and down the lake and the river."

Bates nodded. "Streams were the highways in those days," he said. "Champlain, leading north into the wilderness, and south to Lake George and down the Hudson to the sea, was a magnificent one."

"The Indians called Champlain the Lake-which-is-the-Gateway-to-the-Country. And they called the Otter 'Pecunk-tak,' Crooked River, which it certainly is. There were no permanent Indian settlements in this region, but a lot of tribes used it for summer hunting and trapping grounds."

"It's easy, too, to see *why* the white men came," Bates said. "Soldiers, trappers, adventurers must have had alluring tales to tell of a long lake and lovely fertile valley lying between two great mountain ranges. You say even the Indians recognized it as a good summer resort. After three hundred and fifty years it's still holding its own, isn't it?"

"Samuel de Champlain came down from Quebec in 1609," Kit continued. "He was the first white man to sail past

Split Rock and down through the narrows where we play around in the *Kittyken*. But somewhere south of us, some say at Ticonderoga, some say at Crown Point, about two hundred Iroquois were waiting for him and his small force of Algonquins and Hurons. Champlain fired his arquebus and the Iroquois were frightened by this mysterious thunder and lightning and ran away in a panic. It was a quick, easy victory for Champlain, but from that time on the Iroquois always hated the French."

"Sixteen-nine—" Bates repeated, "that was the year Henry Hudson discovered his river." He turned to Kit. "You really ought to get together with my father. I didn't suspect that your head was so crammed full of history."

"Oh, I came by it the easy way," Kit admitted honestly. "From the time we could toddle, Dad has told Ken and me all kinds of stories about this part of the country where his people settled."

"Did Champlain settle here too?" Bates asked.

"No, he went back to Canada and never revisited the lake that has been named after him. For many years after his visit, French raiding parties from the north and Indians from the south turned the lake into a regular battlefield, so the shores were not very safe for settlers."

"Who was the first hardy soul?"

"Some years after Champlain was here in 1609, the authorities at Albany sent a small force to establish an outpost at a place we call Chimney Point, because after it was destroyed by the French only the chimneys remained. It didn't turn out to be permanent, but it was the first settlement in this region. For fifty years or more the English and the French, with the help of assorted Indian tribes, fought it out

until the French signed a treaty in 1763 giving up all claims
to it. But they kept right on colonizing the lake shore just
the same. Every tenth person around here has a French
name, and the stores in town have signs in their windows
reading '*Ici on parle français.*' There's quite a lot of French-
Canadian folklore and custom mixed in with what the
Yankees brought."

Lines from a habitant poem she and Ken had shouted
every summer during storms at the lake came to Kit and she
added, "Ken and I have a favorite poem in French-Canadian
dialect. It's by a Montreal doctor, William Henry Drummond, and it's called 'The Wreck of the Julie Plante.' It's
about a storm on Lac St. Pierre, but Ken and I always change
the name to Lac Champlain and say it like this:

> *On wan dark night on Lac Champlain*
>   *De win' she blow, blow, blow,*
> *An' de crew of de wood scow* Julie Plante
>   *Got scar't an' run below—*
> *For de win' she blow lak hurricane*
>   *Bimeby she blow some more,*
> *An' de scow bus' up on Lac Champlain*
>   *Wan arpent from de shore.*
>
> *De captinne walk on de fronte deck,*
>   *An' walk de hin' deck too—*
> *He call de crew from up de hole*
>   *He call de cook also.*
> *De cook she's name was Rosie,*
>   *She come from Montreal,*
> *Was chambre maid on lumber barge,*
>   *On de Grande Lachine Canal.*

De win' she blow from nor'-eas'-wes' —
  De sout' win' she blow too.
W'en Rosie cry "Mon cher captinne,
  Mon cher, w'at I shall do?"
Den de Captinne t'row de big ankerre,
  But still the scow she dreef,
De crew he can't pass on de shore,
  Becos' he los' hees skeef.

De night was dark lak' wan black cat,
  De wave run high an' fas',
W'en de captinne tak' de Rosie girl
  An' tie her to de mas'.
Den he also tak' de life preserve,
  An' jump off on de lak',
An' say, "Good-bye, ma Rosie dear,
  I go drown for your sak'."

Nex' morning very early
  'Bout ha'f-pas', two-t'ree-four
De captinne—scow—an' de poor Rosie
  Was corpses on de shore,
For de win' she blow lak' hurricane
  Bimeby she blow some more,
An' de scow bus' up on Lac Champlain
  Wan arpent from de shore.

MORAL

Now all good wood scow sailor man
  Tak' warning by dat storm
An' go an' marry some nice French girl
  An' leev on wan beeg farm.
De win' can blow lak' hurricane
  An' s'pose she blow some more,

You can't get drown on Lac Champlain
So long you stay on shore.

"That's wonderful, Kit," Bates said, laughing without a trace of his earlier bitterness. "You must give me a copy one of these days."

As they made the turn away from the Harbor Club, Kit said, "The French built a fort, too, opposite Chimney Point and called it Fort St. Frédéric. But in 1755 they really went to town when they built that huge one they named Fort Carillon and which is now called Ticonderoga."

"The lake must have been quite a sight then," Bates said, as he slowed down for the turn at the pine tree. "Barges from the south loaded with the household goods of the early settlers. Barges from the north carrying supplies, cannon, ammunition, building materials. French going south, English going north and the Indian canoes gliding in and out among them."

"That's a real pretty picture, but it was the French going south and the English going north, both claiming the same territory, that brought the horrors of the French and Indian War," Kit said crisply. "Finally after Lord Jeffrey Amherst captured Fort Carillon, the French had to give up the lake shores. They burned and destroyed the forts at Ticonderoga and Chimney Point and everything else they had to leave behind, and sailed up the lake for the last time just two hundred years ago, in July 1759. But there was no peace even then because of the struggle between the settlers who had been granted land by the Governor of New Hampshire and the Yorkers who had been given grants to the very same land by the Governor of New York."

"Algonquins and Iroquois, French and English, Yorkers and New Hampshirites," Bates said, "all fighting for the green mountains and valleys of Vermont. Worth fighting for, though, aren't they?"

As they turned in between the gray stone columns at Thendara, he said, smiling at Kit, "This is the shortest trip from town I ever made. Thanks for the first installment of the story of Vergennes, Vermont, and Lake Champlain. You must promise it's 'to be continued.'"

Secretly delighted, Kit laughed deprecatingly. "You should never have let me get started; I suppose I could go on all summer."

"Good," said Bates. "Now, come on up and meet my parents."

Mrs. Cunningham was short and plump, with soft brown eyes and a friendly manner. Mr. Cunningham was tall and thin with deep-set blue eyes like his son's. He rose with his wife to greet Kit. She noticed he had marked with his finger the place in the book he had been reading. Bates excused himself for a moment and returned with a copy of Robert Louis Stevenson's poems which he handed to Kit. She thanked him and said good-by to Mr. and Mrs. Cunningham.

When Bates had left her at her house, Kit rushed up to her bedroom, flung herself on the bed and searched the index of Bates's book for the poem. There it was. "Romance," page fifty-eight.

She read it through, lingering over the last verse:

And this shall be for music when no one else is near,
The fine song for singing, the rare song to hear!

That only I remember, that only you admire,
Of the broad road that stretches and the roadside fire.

Kit read the poem again and then fell back on the pil-
lows. "That only I remember," she repeated dreamily, "that
only you admire . . ." Oh, Bates, her heart cried, admire *me*
a little, just a little, please.

9

An Unexpected Meeting

It became the custom for the same group of young people, more or less, to meet each morning at the Cunninghams' to play tennis. Bates was usually on hand, but if he was not, they knew he wanted them to use the courts just the same. Once or twice he spent considerable time talking to Kit about the fascination of this part of Lake Champlain, where so much that was stirring and exciting had taken place in the past.

But he spent just as much time talking with Joan or Jane and even more with Elaine. He even seemed to enjoy Ah-Ting, and the baby talk that Elaine lavished on the small dog apparently amused rather than disgusted him.

After tennis, the crowd usually went swimming. Bates did not take part in the diving contests, but he could keep up with any of them in swimming. He made an agreeable passenger in whatever boat was towing the water skiers, amiably helping to fish out the casualties.

Kit's grace and splendid coordination made her the undisputed star of this sport. She was a delight to watch. No matter what the speed or the twists and turns of the boat,

she never took a spill, as she balanced like some lovely flying goddess, her hair blown back by the breeze.

Early Saturday morning, Kit drove to Burlington with her mother to meet her father, who had finally straightened out the textile client and was able to get away for the weekend.

"It's one of my blue days," Kit said happily, "when the world is painted by Picasso with his blue palette in his hand."

It had rained during the night, but the wind had shifted in the early morning and was blowing gently now from the north. The mountains stood out clear and sharp against the incredible deep blue of the sky, framing the indigo sheet of the lake. As they turned up toward Vergennes, the Adirondacks piled up in the west, range in back of range, massed in shades of blue, lavender, periwinkle, and gray. Then the Green Mountains came into view in the east, softer, more rounded and deeply blue—Camel's Hump, Lincoln, Mansfield—serene and friendly.

Kit remembered a schoolmate of her mother's, just returned from a trip to the coast which had included many of the national parks, who had said, "The Rockies are majestic, awe-inspiring, but the Green Mountains are so comfortable and friendly." Kit had read somewhere that they, together with the White Mountains and the Appalachians, were the oldest mountains in the country, older than the Rockies. When the glaciers had swept over this part of the country, they had scraped the White Mountains bare in places, leaving them rocky and craggy, but passed gently over the Green, leaving them softly wooded to their tops.

Vergennes no longer had train service. The Rutland Railroad, unable to withstand the competition of the motor car and truck, had at last capitulated, as the steamers *Vermont* and *Ticonderoga,* which had formerly made daily circuits of the lake, had earlier been forced to do.

Now the "Ti," so beloved by everyone up and down the shores of Lake Champlain, was high and dry, a relic of bygone days on the green lawn of Shelburne Museum. Kit had heard stories about the "Ti" all her life. In her childhood, she had known the side-wheeler's regular daily trips and had waved to her on her last gallant excursions. She was thankful that the steamer had been saved from destruction and was lying safe in Shelburne Museum.

Some of the railroad stations along the Rutland right of way had been turned into stores or restaurants, and passengers for the Champlain Valley had to seek other means of transportation. Mr. Turner had come up from the city on the Central Vermont and would come over to Burlington on the bus.

When Kit and her mother reached the Queen City, they walked up and down Church Street, looking at the shop windows while they waited. Kit was surprised to find herself taking a genuine interest in the displays of dresses.

"This one would be becoming to you, Kit," her mother said, stopping to admire a pale blue tailored dress. "The lines are excellent. If we had time you might try it on."

Kit wondered if Bates liked blue and what scrap of poetry he would quote for her if she were wearing the blue dress in the window. She could hardly believe that she was actually sorry not to have time to try on a dress!

She could not keep Bates out of everything she thought or did. She could not hear music, thrill to one of Champlain's dramatic sunsets without thinking of him. Usually she would have waited contentedly, happy to be meeting her father. Now she was impatient for him to arrive only so that she could get back in time to see Bates at the tennis courts.

"I hope your father will be able to stay a few days," Mrs. Turner said, as they turned back toward the hotel. "Of course I'm glad he's successful, but sometimes I wonder if it's worth it, working day and night the way he does, never able to plan ahead with certainty for vacations or other free time as other people do. If they telephone him from the office over the weekend, I've a good mind to take the call and not tell him anything about it."

"Oh, Mother, you wouldn't," Kit protested.

Mrs. Turner laughed. "Well, I'd like to. Sometimes I think I'd rather eke out an existence on a worn-out farm or in a city tenement and have a little of my husband's companionship."

It must be hard on Mother, Kit thought with new perceptiveness. Several times a week, Miss Westley, her father's secretary, called to say that Mr. Turner couldn't make it for dinner. Often dates had to be canceled, plans changed at the last minute just as had happened about coming up to the lake this year, because, her mother said bitterly, some tempermental client had to have his hand held. It must be lonely for Mother when Dad couldn't get home in the evenings and she and Ken were busy with their own affairs.

"Maybe Dad will have some definite news about a real vacation," she said, giving her mother's arm a little pat. "You might even be able to go away together for a cruise or a little trip to Canada or something." Impelled to sacrifice by this new sympathy with her mother, she added generously, "Ken and I could stay with Aunt Charlotte."

"Honey, wouldn't that be simply magnificent!" Mrs. Turner exclaimed with the extravagant enthusiasm of a teen-ager. Then she made a little face. "But your Father will only say, 'Next year, Sal, just wait till next year, and we'll take a good long vacation—a month or so.' He's been saying that for the last three years, ever since they made him a vice-president. Look, isn't that Bates Cunningham coming down the street?"

Kit's heart began pounding dizzily as Bates limped toward them.

"Why, Mrs. Turner," he said, stopping in surprise. "Hello, Kit. What brings you to Burlington at this hour of the morning?"

"That man in the tan suit just getting out of the bus across the street," Mrs. Turner said. "Come over and meet my husband, Bates."

"And how about you?" Kit heard herself saying easily as they crossed the street. "What are you doing in town so bright and early?"

"I had to pick up some books at MacAuliffe's for Dad. I wanted to get it over with early and have the day free. It's such a perfect one, I'd like to do a little exploring and I need a good guide. How about getting a lunch together and going off on a sightseeing junket with me? Would you mind missing the tennis and the swimming?"

Kit bobbed her head enthusiastically at Bates, as she greeted her father.

"How's my sweet Kate?" Richard Turner turned from his wife to give Kit a hug and kiss.

"Dick, this is Bates Cunningham, our next-door neighbor. The Cunninghams have taken Thendara for the summer."

"Welcome to our circle, Bates." Mr. Turner shook hands heartily. He was a big genial man with the sandy hair, brows, and lashes Kit had inherited. His ruddy complexion and expansive air of abounding health and energy made Bates appear even paler and thinner by contrast.

They talked for a few minutes, and Bates took his leave. "I'll deliver my package, pick up some lunch, and be over for you about eleven," he told Kit. "Thanks for being willing to show me around."

"Never mind about lunch," Kit said. "I'll fix something."

Mrs. Turner looked pleased. Kit could almost read her thoughts—"A boy for Kit, dates at last, thank goodness!" But her mother only said, gazing after Bates, "He's a charming boy."

They had passed Shelburne Museum with the "Ti" standing proud against the sky, and the covered bridge, complete with horse and buggy. Her father turned and spoke to Kit, who was dreaming in the back seat.

"How goes it this summer, honey? Having fun?"

"Sure, good crowd, a lot of swimming, but Dad," she launched again into an old complaint, "I don't see why I can't take the *Kittyken* out by myself. I can manage her just as well as Ken can—maybe better—and I know the lake just as well. What if he is two years older? I'm almost fifteen and plenty old enough to be trusted with a boat."

"Do we have to fight this out every time I come up?" Dick Turner asked wearily. "You know as well as I do the kind of storms that come up in the twinkling of an eye on Lake Champlain. I wouldn't have a minute's peace in the city if I thought you were running around alone in the *Kittyken*. You can never tell what a girl of your age would do in an emergency—lose her head probably. I know you can run the boat, and it's all right when Ken is with you, but you are not to take her out by yourself. Understand, Katharine?"

"Oh, Dad," Kit said. "There's no fun in running the boat with you or Ken standing by, as if I were just a kid of six. You have such funny old-fashioned ideas about girls, you remind me of Aunt Charlotte."

"Never mind about Aunt Charlotte," said her mother. "You might find her ideas not so bad one of these days. I agree with her that a woman should be a woman and proud of it, no matter what she does or how successful she is."

For the rest of the ride Kit was silent. She wasn't sulking, for that was not her way, but she was thinking hard. She was disappointed about being refused permission to run the boat, because she had thought of taking Bates to Diamond Island, where Captain Kidd was said to have buried treasure, and soldiers had hidden in Revolutionary times; or to Button Bay, where the Indians had camped in summer to make their bowls and pitchers from its clay; or to Arnold's Bay, where the wily Benedict had burned his ships, and where their rotting hulls could sometimes be seen on still, clear days.

But that would have to wait. Her father had so little time to be with them at the lake, a spot he loved even more than she did. She would not spoil his weekend by continually nagging. Right under their very noses, she thought, I'm changing, growing up a little, and they don't even see it.

10

A Picnic for Two

Kit jumped out of the car as it came to a stop and dashed into the kitchen.

"Martha," she squealed in high excitement, "I'm going on a picnic with Bates Cunningham. I've less than an hour to get ready. What can I fix in a hurry for lunch?"

Martha moved leisurely out of the huge pantry closet with its great butchers' ice boxes. In the horse-and-buggy days of Kit's great-grandfather they had been filled with giant cakes of ice, cut in winter from the lake and stored in the sawdust-filled icehouse. Provisions had been kept there for long periods of time. "Well, ain't that nice now?" Martha said. "Just you and Bates, Kit?"

Kit nodded. "How about deviled eggs? May I have some of the meat loaf for sandwiches and a couple of pieces of that cake you just made?"

"You bet. I'll serve the cake in slices for supper and no one'll know the difference. Where're you goin'?"

"We met Bates in Burlington." Kit was aware that she would have to satisfy Martha's friendly interest. "He wants me to show him some of the special spots around here. Will you devil the eggs while I make the sandwiches?"

"You bet."

They went to work, Martha's calm deliberation contrasting with Kit's feverish frenzy.

"Bates seems like a nice fellow," Martha said as they worked. "Too bad he's so lame."

Kit paused in her operation of spreading butter very generously on a piece of bread. "Do you know, I never think of it any more." It was true. His limp was a part of Bates that she accepted without particular notice, though she was always aware of his deep blue eyes shadowed by those very long lashes, or the rich music of his voice.

"Ain't he a mite old for you?" Martha asked, stirring seasoning into the egg yolks. "Somehow he don't seem your type either, Kit."

"Oh, I don't know," Kit answered airily, but she admitted to herself it was strange she should feel the way she did about a boy who would lose an oar and not even bother to retrieve it, who quoted poetry at the drop of a hat, and could join in so few of the sports she loved.

Unlike the Kit of old, she was so fussy about the appearance of the lunch, the color of the napkins, the way it was packed, that Martha drove her out of the kitchen. "Go on, get yourself fixed up. Your nose is shiny. I'll finish this."

Kit took a quick shower, splashed herself lavishly with cologne, put on her brown Bermudas with her favorite aqua shirt. For once her hair behaved well, hugging her head in soft rust-colored waves. She couldn't do anything about the pale gold of her brows and lashes she hated so or the freckles across her pert little nose, but she took special pains with her new pink lipstick. She was just ready when Bates turned into the driveway.

She ran quickly down the dark stairs, grabbed up the lunch as she dashed through the kitchen, tossing a thank-you kiss at Martha as she passed.

"Which way, Madame Conductor?" Bates asked when they were heading down the driveway.

"Bristol Gap," Kit replied promptly. "I thought we could eat our lunch at the falls."

He drove the car up the road to Vergennes. The lake rippled lazily behind them. Between the pale blue backdrop of the distant Adirondacks and the soft deep blue of the Green Mountains, the wide Champlain Valley stretched serene and peaceful in the bright sunlight. The rolling pastures, dotted with herds of black and white cattle, were an orange, yellow, and white mosaic of devil's-paintbrush, buttercups, and daisies, with the purple of vetch massed against the gray satin of stump and rail fences. Here and there the white needle spire of a church pricked the deep blue of the sky, and great barns were broad splashes of red against the green, with small white farmhouses nestling nearby.

"On a day like this you can understand why men braved the wilderness to settle here," Bates said. "This lovely valley must have looked mighty pleasant. Streams and lakes for fishing and for mill power. Lumber for building and for potash . . ."

"And a short growing season for crops," Kit said, pricking his poet's dream, "with a long, cold, snow-bound winter to follow."

Bates shrugged. "That's when they did their lumbering, fishing, hunting, and trapping. It was a rugged life but it built strong, independent, self-sufficient men."

Kit, reveling in the wide expanse of farmland stretching

to the distant mountains, said, "It's so typically New England on a Summer Day, like a landscape by Luigi Lucioni or Winslow Homer."

She amused Bates with a tale of her father's that had delighted her as a child. He had told her that in Vermont the legs of the cattle were shorter on one side than the other so that they could get around the steep hills better—and she had even believed him once!

When they passed a flock of sheep, unusual now among the cattle, she explained that once this part of the state had been noted for sheep raising.

"Ken's planning to get a flock," she said, "so he won't have to mow our grass."

Bristol, a tiny town at the foot of Mount Lincoln, with its wide uncluttered Main Street, its village green and charming old inn dating back to 1793, had an air of serenity and strength. At Kit's direction, Bates turned up toward the gorge and falls. Kit showed him the huge boulder on which, back in 1891, a Dr. Joseph C. Greene of Buffalo, New York, had carefully cut the Lord's Prayer in three-inch letters which were always kept freshly painted white, and she told him the various legends she had heard about it.

Soon they heard the sound of rushing, tumbling water, and Bates parked the car just off the road above the falls. As they followed the path through the woods to the rim of the gorge, Bates carrying the picnic basket, they realized from the sound of shouts and laughter that they were not to be alone.

The tree-crowned rocky sides of the gorge rose steeply wall-like about thirty feet on either side of a swift stream, dashing madly in small showers of spray around huge boulders or flowing crystal clear over the sandy bottom. The sun, slanting through the trees, struck jewels from the dancing spray of the falls and pierced in golden shafts to the brown pebbly bottom of the wide, deep pool at the foot of the falls.

Thirty feet above the pool on the flat, overhanging gray rocks, a group of shouting boys was clustered, their sturdy brown bodies bare except for the faded, mended shorts they wore as bathing trunks.

"Aw, go on, Clint, you promised," the smallest one was pleading. "Go on, swing me over."

"Can't you wait a minute, kid?" one of the taller boys said. "Don't get excited. There's plenty of time."

Kit and Bates, approaching from an angle, could see that the big boulder stuck out shelflike, forming a sort of roof over an indented ledge of rock just below. Kit's toes curled, as the big boy lowered his body over the edge, hung for a moment in space and swung in to land on the ledge. He stood there a moment and then, plummeting down through the air, cut cleanly through the water of the pool.

Kit let out the breath she had been holding and released Bates's arm which she had clutched in her excitement. "What a beautiful dive!" she breathed in admiration for the boy's skill and courage. "But how did he ever dare try it! It makes me think of pictures I have seen of boys diving off Diamond Head or some volcano, or whatever it is, in Hawaii."

"Those crazy kids are risking their necks," Bates said. "But I don't think it would do any good for *me* to try to stop them," he added wryly.

Of course not, Kit thought in quick sympathy. The boys would only ignore Bates as a timid, fuddy-duddy spoilsport, if he limped down to remonstrate with them. With her heart yearning to comfort him, she stood stupidly silent.

One after another the three big boys dived expertly into the pool, while the smallest one clamored to be allowed to try it. The second in size climbed like a monkey over the overhanging rocks and up into the trees growing out of the boulders edging the chasm. He caught sight of Bates and Kit and ran to tell the others. From then on the boys, conscious of an audience, swaggered in even greater daring.

"We'd better go about our business and ignore them," Bates suggested. "Apparently they're accustomed to this hair-brained stunt. They'll be all right, if they don't have to outdo themselves to impress us."

Kit agreed. "Let's eat." She took the basket and began to lay out the lunch, spreading the cloth on a flat rock about a hundred yards from the boys' natural high-diving platform.

Bates tasted his egg and bit into a sandwich. "My dear young woman," he said solemnly. "This is too much for one girl—a poem on the tennis court, a goddess on water skis—and now a *Cordon Bleu* cook with sense enough to make a man-sized sandwich. This meat loaf is food for the gods. And what is that unusual seasoning in the eggs?"

Kit was strongly tempted to accept his compliments as Elaine had those she had won for her cake, but she was too honest.

"I hate to do it," she said, "but I have to admit that I had no more to do with this lunch than just putting the sandwiches together. Martha made the meat loaf, deviled the eggs, and baked the cake."

She could feel her face stiffen a little as she registered determination to dog Martha's heels every spare moment until she learned to cook. Then she giggled. "Alackaday, this is none of I!" she said to herself and thought how amazed her mother, Aunt Charlotte, and even Ken would be.

With a sandwich halfway to her mouth, she froze. The smallest boy had at last won his point. The two biggest boys, holding him by the arms, were swinging him out over the gorge. Involuntarily Kit jumped up, running silently forward. She did not dare call out for fear of startling them. Behind her, Bates had drawn himself awkwardly to his feet. Before Kit could reach them, the boys lowered the youngster over the edge. His feet flailed wildly for a moment, then he landed in a heap on the ledge. He scrambled to his feet, raised his arms and plunged down into the pool. Kit, clinging to a tree on the edge of the gorge, did not breathe until she saw his tow head bob up to the surface.

The second smallest boy ran toward her. "Guy did it," he shouted proudly. "Guy did it!"

"I saw him," Kit said drily.

"How long have you boys been using this for a diving board?" Bates asked.

"Since we moved to Bristol. But Guy never tried it before."

"He might have broken his neck," Bates said sternly. "What do you boys know about the depth and the bottom of that pool?"

"Shucks, there's nothing to worry about, mister. The Bristol kids have always dived from here into this swimming hole."

He told them his name was Johnny; that Guy, who was seven, was his younger brother. "I'm nine," he said. "I can't swim but I can climb anything. They call me Monkey because I can climb trees and all sorts of places where the rest of them are too scared to try." He was thinner, quicker, more wiry than the others. His hazel eyes danced in his alert little face. The two blond boys, Allan, ten, and Clinton, twelve, were his older brothers, he told them; the dark ones, Jim LeBeau and Pete Dubois, were friends.

He accepted with grown-up dignity the sandwich Kit offered, thanking her gravely. When Guy had scrambled up the tortuous ascent he came over to join his brother.

"There was nothing to it, Monkey," he boasted, his face beaming. "I said I'd do it and I did. If the big boys can do it, I can do it."

He was shorter than Johnny, stocky and sturdy. The small boys called to the others to come over and be introduced. The big boys held back self-consciously, but they finally joined the party. All the brothers had blond hair and big hazel eyes. They were handsome boys, with clean-cut features. Though their swimming trunks were old, they were clean and well mended. Their tanned bodies were well-cared for.

Kit and Bates divided the lunch with them. They were scrupulously polite. Even though it was a picnic, it was evident that someone had taken pains with their table manners.

Their mother must be a fine person, Kit thought. But I wonder if she knows how dangerous their swimming hole is.

They finished the lunch in short order. Kit repacked the basket. When she spoke about careless picnickers spoiling beautiful spots like this by leaving a trail of trash, the younger boys scrambled around collecting every scrap of paper in sight. Laughing, Kit knew that she was carrying home much more than her own sandwich wrappings.

Monkey came to sit beside Kit, cuddling close to her side on the big flat rock.

"We only moved to Bristol in the early spring," Guy was telling Bates, "Monkey, my mother and me. Allan and Clint are staying with my mother's aunt in Panton. They don't like it much over there so every chance they get they come over here to spend the day. We sure like this swimmin' hole."

"We're aimin' to go back to Vergennes next winter," Allan said, "if only my mother can find a job and a place to live. Monkey and I miss Allan and Clint something awful and we want to live all together again in our own house."

"You lived in Vergennes?" Kit asked. "What's your name?"

"Howard," Guy answered for him. "I'm Guy Howard."

Kit's heart skipped a beat. These handsome well-brought-up boys must be sons of the man who had lost his life on the ice floe. Their mother was the woman she had seen at the library—Molly Howard. She must be a grand mother —her boys were proof of that—but what a task for a woman to bring up seven youngsters all by herself!

Monkey had been gazing at Kit admiringly. "Is she your girl, mister?" he asked.

Kit felt herself blushing fiery red.

Bates laughed. "What do you think of my taste, son? Pretty good, huh?"

"She's awful pretty," Monkey said. "And nice too."

11

Kit Launches a Project

For the rest of the day the Howards haunted Kit. The boys were so appealing. Monkey, with his quick movements and bright, teasing eyes. Guy, sturdy and straightforward, bent on attempting whatever the older boys did. All of them, so attractive and alert, so polite and well-cared for. Her one short glimpse of Molly Howard had given Kit the feeling that here was a woman strong and brave and proud. But how could she bring up seven children without help?

Sitting on the grass at the side of the court at Thendara next morning, she was watching Jane and Bud give Joan and Ken a hard fight, but her mind was still on the Howards. When Ray put his hand on her arm, she gave a startled jump.

"Three times I speak to the lady, and she ignores me," Ray complained. "Perhaps it's a hearing aid you need, Brick Top? Or just to return from outer space?"

"I didn't mean to ignore you," Kit said tartly, "but you don't have to scare me to death, do you?"

Elaine perked up Ah-Ting's blue bow, which matched the skirt and sweater she was wearing, and giggled.

"Outer space, pooh," she disposed of such nonsense with an airy little gesture. "Kit was probably dreaming about a handsome boy friend she left back in the city."

"Why not one she has recently met right here?" Bates said. "I'm available."

"Say it isn't so, Brick Top," Ray implored, gesturing dramatically. "Say you're true to me. I'm too young for a blighted life."

Kit could feel herself blushing as usual, but she managed feebly to enter into their teasing.

"Sorry. Not my day for suitors," she said, shaking her head. "Applicants interviewed Tuesdays and Fridays by appointment only."

Elaine, fondling Ah-Ting, cradled in her lap, looked surprised, as if she were thinking, "Don't tell me I'm going to have competition from Ken's little sister."

Ray pulled a penny from his pocket and offered it to Kit. "Well then, I'll buy," he said. "What *were* you thinking about so seriously?"

"The Howards," Kit confessed. "I can't seem to get them out of my mind."

She told them the story she had learned from Martha, ending with a glowing description of the boys and her feeling about Molly Howard.

"I wish there were something I could do," she said. "Some way really to help them."

"Maybe we could raise some money among the summer people," Elaine suggested. "We could give a benefit of some kind."

"We might run a tennis tournament, with admission fees and prizes, or put on a water ballet," Ray said. "The guests at the Harbor Club and Rockledge would probably come. People might even come over from Westport."

"You couldn't run much of a tournament with only a couple of courts," Bates objected. "But the water ballet idea is interesting. We might have an afternoon of various water sports—outboard motor races, canoe jousting, water skiing, ending up with the ballet. We could charge general admission for the spectators and entrance fees for each event."

Elaine had been blowing Ah-Ting's silky ears, cooing, "Was him toe tweet, toe loving?" Now she sat up so suddenly that she spilled the outraged little dog off her lap. "Why don't we put on a play, or tableaux—you know, something like that charade party the Gunnersons gave a couple of years ago."

"Count me out of any stunt like that," Ray said emphatically.

"But it would be such fun," Elaine protested plaintively. "You're all always playing tennis and swimming or racing around the lake. The play would be something different."

Kit saw the look of understanding sympathy on Bates's face. There was not much Elaine could do in the line of water sports, but no one could doubt that she would be the star of any tableaux or play they might choose.

"We might make more money with a play, at that," Bates said thoughtfully. "People go for summer theater in a big way."

Elaine leaned forward eagerly, the sunlight gleaming on the pale silver gilt of her hair. Her round china-blue eyes were open wide. She looks like a doll under somebody's Christmas tree, Kit thought.

"Oh, please, Bates," Elaine begged. "Let's do the play." She turned to Kit and Ray. "Do you know that Bates is planning to take a drama workshop course next fall? He could write an original play for us. Wouldn't that be exciting?"

Kit felt a twinge of that disturbed feeling she had experienced before. How did Elaine know so much about Bates's plans? She shook her head, and turned her mind resolutely to the benefit, deliberately refusing to harbor troublesome thoughts. It would be wonderful if Bates wrote a play they could produce before a real live audience. Suppose Elaine were the star? She and Bates were really so decent about sitting on the sidelines cheering while the others performed that it was only fair that they should have a chance to shine.

She smiled at Ray. "The water sports thing is a wonderful idea and we really ought to do it sometime," she said, surprised at her new-found tactfulness, "but don't you think the play might make more money for the Howards?"

"Oh, I do," Elaine put in eagerly. "I really do. We might even run it for two or three nights."

"It would mean a lot more work," Bates warned, "at least for the actors. Running it, promotion and all that, would be about the same."

"I don't mind a little work in a good cause," Ray said, "but don't expect me to get up on a stage and speak any lines."

"What goes on here?" Ken demanded, as he and the others, puffing and mopping their faces, joined the group under the trees. "What's with this huddle that's so important you guys don't even applaud a hard-fought victory?"

"Oh, Ken, we're sorry," Kit cried in contrition. "Who won?"

"What a gallery!" Ken said in disgust. He took Joan's hand and bowed. "Meet the winnahs—and I don't mind telling you we had tough competition."

"You were just wonderful," Elaine said automatically, her words for all of them, her eyes making the tribute for Ken alone. "Oh, Ken," she went on, "we've been working out a marvelous plan. Wait till you hear."

Interrupting each other, sometimes all talking at once, Elaine, Kit, Bates, and Ray gave the tennis players the complete story of the Howards and the money-raising project for their benefit.

Joan and Jane were enthusiastic, but it took considerable persuasion to enlist the reluctant cooperation of Bud and Ken. Like Ray, they took a dim view of amateur theatricals. Elaine's charming wheedling and Kit's earnest pleading finally wore them down. It was agreed that if Bates could come up with an idea within the next day or so for some sort of a performance that would not demand too much memorizing of lines or too many rehearsals, they would go along with it.

The performance would take place at Thendara of course, where the Gunnersons had held their charade parties. Only a couple of steps divided the living room from the dining room below and the living room would make a grand stage. On either side of the fireplace doors opened into guest wings that would make wonderful dressing rooms and right and left entrances. The beautiful winding staircase at the right could also be used, as well as the porch doors on the left.

"I'll paint scenery, take tickets, pepper the country with billboards," Ray said again, "but don't ask me to act. Not even for you, Brick Top, light of my life."

But Kit, once again completely absorbed in her own thoughts, did not hear him. She had just been struck by a brilliant idea. Why not do a sort of pageant—tableaux mostly, with maybe a few people having a line or two to say—about the history of Vermont and Lake Champlain in general and of Vergennes in particular? Bates would be the narrator of course. His voice was perfect for that sort of thing. She could help him with the local scenes which she had known about since she was a child. Elaine would be the star naturally and the focus of his attention in re-hearsals, but Kit would be sort of his girl Friday in the actual writing of the script.

Excitedly she began to outline her idea. Bates was inter-ested at once, as she had hoped he would be.

"That's not a bad idea, Kit," he said, "it should be a lot of fun and not too much work to knock together."

Kit thought of Ken or Ray finding the writing of a his-torical pageant "a lot of fun" and almost giggled. What was one man's meat was another's poison, all right, she thought tritely, but the bromide had never before held so much meaning for her. She was beginning to see that there was nothing so very dreadful about being one's self, no matter how different from the rest of the crowd, instead of trying so hard to be a carbon copy of everyone else, as she had last year when she had been a silly little freshman.

Ken and Ray approved because they could see themselves as pioneers, hunters, soldiers, or Indians, with few lines to memorize.

"And it should interest both the summer visitors and the people who live here all year 'round," Ken added.

The tennis session broke up then, and the group dispersed to change into swimming togs and meet again at the Turners' dock in half an hour.

"In return for the loan of your Stevenson book, I'll trade you my grandfather's history of Addison County," Kit told Bates. "You'll find a lot of local stuff in it. I'll give it to you when you come over later."

Kit jumped out of the car almost before Ken had stopped it and burst through the back door. She grabbed Martha around her ample waist and whirled her around the kitchen, chanting:

Hooray! Hooray! Hooray!
We're going to put on a play
To garner the lucre to pay
For a house for the Howards some day.
Hooray! Hooray! Hooray!

"Kit," protested Martha, puffing and pulling away. "What's got into you anyway?"

"Just another brainstorm." Ken followed his sister into the kitchen. "Kit had a bright idea, and its unaccustomed brilliance has addled her brains."

"It's a wonderful idea," Kit said happily. "We're going to put on a play for the benefit of the Howards. If we raise a thousand dollars, we could buy that little house out by the poor farm for them, so they can come back to Vergennes and Mrs. Howard can get a job at Fisher's."

"For Pete's sake, Kit, take it easy," Ken protested. "You'll never raise a thousand dollars with an amateur stunt like this."

Almost simultaneously, Martha exclaimed, "Bless your heart, Kit, that'd be wonderful. But Molly Howard is plenty proud and independent. She'd accept money from the Veterans because Will was one, but she'd hate to be an object of charity to summer people."

Kit, already scurrying through the living room to the front porch where her father and mother and Aunt Charlotte were sitting, paid no attention.

"Guess what!" she shouted. "We're going to put on a play for the Howards."

It was only when she saw the expression on Aunt Charlotte's face that she realized her state of dishevelment. Her shirt was wrinkled and damp with perspiration from a stiff set of singles she had played with Ray; her shorts were dirty from sitting on the grass while they talked over the exciting plan for the Howards; she could feel that her face was shiny with perspiration and probably streaked with dirt.

"Still the same Katharine, I see," Aunt Charlotte said coolly. "You look as if your morning had been a violent one to say the least."

Kit, reading Aunt Charlotte's mind, could almost hear her adding to herself, "No wonder the boys don't date Kit. Elaine would never permit herself to be seen in such a state. Poor Sally Belle!"

Her father knocked the ashes out of the pipe he reserved for use at the lake. "What's all this about a play?"

Ken, his mouth full of cupcake purloined from Martha, let the screen door slam behind him. "Only a little matter of a thousand dollars. Kit's going to raise it by giving a play."

Dick Turner whistled. "A thousand dollars!" He waved his hand. "Just like that, huh?"

"Listen, Daddy," Kit went over to sit on the arm of his Adirondack chair. "You know about Will Howard. Well, we met his sons over at Bristol Falls the other day. They're darling boys and so well brought up and polite, you just know they must have a wonderful mother. I think we summer people ought to do something to help them."

Her father put his arm around her. "My sweet Kate," he said. "Good for you! What exactly do you propose to do?"

Kit explained about the play, the house in Vergennes, and the possible job for Mrs. Howard.

"Go ahead with your plans, Kitten," said her father. "When I come back next week, we'll talk about promotion. I'll help with that, and we'll make a stab at that thousand."

"*If* your father gets back next week," Mrs. Turner put in, adding bitterly," I wish I were married to an ordinary husband instead of an indispensable man. The office called a little while ago. It is strange to me that an advertising firm as large as Ogden and Peters can't manage without your father for a few days. He has to leave again right after church tomorrow."

"I'm awfully sorry, Sal," Dick Turner said placatingly, "I hate to spoil your plans again, but if Evans is coming to town on Monday, I've simply got to be there. You know what a big deal that oil account is. I can't afford to have anything go wrong. I'll do my best to get off next Friday for a couple of weeks, I promise you."

He acts almost guilty, Kit thought, as if the call back to town were for some selfish pleasure of his own. Knowing how he loved this part of the country where he had been born and where he had grown up, she thought her mother's attitude must make it doubly hard for him. She sighed. It was hard for her mother too, never to be sure when or for how long she could have her husband's companionship; waiting dinner in the city for a man whose secretary called at the last minute to say he couldn't make it; spending lonely weekends when he was out of town and long summers at the lake when he came to stay and was called right back to the city.

"Going to use the *Kittyken* this afternoon, Dad?" Ken inquired.

"Ask your mother," his father answered. "I'm devoting this afternoon to my best girl."

"I suppose you'd like to go fishing with Ken," Sally Turner said, "and I ought to be big enough to urge you to go ahead, but I'm so selfish I want you to myself on the rare occasions when you are around."

"Suppose we ride over and take a look at that cutter bar Ed Horton has for sale. Then I'll take you to dinner at the Dogteam Tavern or anywhere you say."

"Good," Ken said, relieved. "I didn't want to go fishing. I'd like to take Elaine over to Westport."

"Dad," Kit began. She was about to tease again for permission to take out the *Kittyken* by herself. More than ever now, she wanted to take Bates in the boat to see some of the legendary places around Vergennes and up and down the lake and river. She bit back the words. It was bad enough for her father to have to go back to the city and face her mother's disappointment without having to bear the added irritation of his daughter's endless whining and teasing. She said instead, "Thanks, Dad, for offering to help in promoting the play. We'll hold you to it. We have to make this the biggest event ever held on the Vermont shore of Lake Champlain."

"Oh, throw in the New York shore too," Ken urged airily. "Don't be chicken."

Kit paid no attention to him. She was lost in surprise at her own behavior. This business of seeing her mother and father as individuals with virtues and faults, hopes and fears, sorrows and joys of their own was amazingly new to her.

I'm different somehow this summer, she thought. Maybe I am beginning to grow up. I can see it has its good points and bad. I'm not quite sure I like it, but I know one thing, child or woman, before the summer's over, I'm going to run the *Kittyken* . . . and help earn a house for Molly Howard . . . and wear that aqua formal on a date with Bates Cunningham . . . I hope—I hope!

12

Ticonderoga

Bates was now spending most of his time researching and writing, with Kit as his willing assistant. Her family were outspoken in their astonishment.

"What gives?" Ken remarked in amazement. "I never thought these tired old eyes of mine would witness Kit giving up high dives for history. Beats me." And he walked off shaking his head.

Several times during the next week, Kit and Bates, in the Jaguar, visited places connected in one way or another with interesting events of the past. On the morning on which they were to run down to Crown Point and Ticonderoga, Kit was surprised to find Elaine in the car when Bates stopped for her.

"Think of it," Elaine said, her high voice shrill with shocked emphasis, "all the times I've visited at the lake and I've never been to Ticonderoga!"

Kit could not escape the thought that no one as attractive as Bates had ever been making a trip to the old fort during one of Elaine's visits. She made a valiant effort to hide her discomfiture as she took her place on the front seat beside

Elaine, who was neatly installed in the middle. Elaine kept up an almost constant chatter, and Kit had no opportunity to talk with Bates about history or anything else.

While they were crossing the bridge to the New York shore, Bates said, with a quick glance up the expanse of blue water, broken only by a graceful white pleasure cruiser and a big lumbering barge, propelled by a puffing tug, "There must have been a lot more traffic on the lake while the French were building Ticonderoga, since they were forced to bring most of their supplies down from Canada."

"What did the French call the fort?" Elaine asked. "I know you told me, but I've forgotten."

"Fort Carillon because the rushing falls nearby sounded like bells," Bates told her. Then he added, "You can see why both France and England wanted to possess Champlain. What did you tell me the Indians called it, Kit? Gateway to the Country? You can see that whoever controlled the lake could hold all the rich surrounding country. So back in 1755, some twenty years before the American Revolution, the Marquis de Vaudreuil, Governor General of New France, commissioned a great engineer, Michel Chartres, to build him a fort which would command the lake. Chartres leveled off the top of a stony promontory, dominating the lake both north and south, and used the stone to build a great, star-shaped fortress. Just imagine the hustle and bustle that must have resounded in the quiet wilderness with some two thousand men cutting timber, quarrying stone, and building the outer works and barracks."

"Imagine," Elaine echoed feebly, and Kit thought with an inward giggle that she looked as though she regretted her question.

Wickedly Kit egged Bates on, "And after all their back-breaking work, how long did the French hold the fort?"

"Only about four years. In 1759, after a three-day fight, Lord Jeffrey Amherst captured it from a small force that had been left there when most of the French army returned to Quebec. Before they fled, the French destroyed practically everything they could get their hands on."

"But the British rebuilt Fort Carillon into what they thought was an impregnable stronghold, and christened it Ticonderoga," Kit contributed. "And they also ordered Lord Jeffrey to build a fort at Crown Point at a cost of about ten million dollars, which was certainly a terrific sum for those days."

Determinedly Elaine began to sing "Lord Jeffrey Amherst," and pretty soon Bates and Kit joined in, as they swooped around a curve into the little park at Crown Point where a monument to Champlain was erected in 1909.

Atop a lofty stone pedestal the great explorer, in helmet and breastplate, gazes up the lake that bears his name. Bates copied the inscription:

> 1609   SAMUEL CHAMPLAIN   1909
> INTREPID NAVIGATOR
> SCHOLARLY EXPLORER
> CHRISTIAN PIONEER

A narrow staircase wound up through the base to the great light at the top. Bates, in spite of his lameness, insisted on going up to enjoy the fine view of the lake. Kit went ahead, winding up through the dark, narrow passageway, her feet clattering on the metal stairs. Elaine followed, counting the steps and gasping when she reached the top that she would never have started up if she had known there were seventy-six steps.

Kit thought the view of the surrounding country and up and down the lake was worth seventy-six steps, but Elaine said crossly that the lake looked just the same from her own dock.

After a few minutes they made their way down again and went over to the gray stone ruins of Lord Jeffrey's fort.

"It must have been a comfort to those early trappers and settlers to know they had these great stone forts to support them," Bates said as they wandered through room after room in the two long, two-story rectangles of gray stone. The roofs and floors were long since gone and grass and weeds carpeted the long rows of rooms.

Bates was interested in the thickness of the walls, the shape of the windows. Kit, counting the innumerable fireplaces both upstairs and down, thought that even with so many, the soldiers—she could almost see them running up and down the gray stone stairs in their red coats—must have spent many an uncomfortable night in winter.

A bronze tablet, which Bates read aloud, stated: "Fort Crown Point Built by General Amherst in 1759 to safeguard British interests in North America Captured by Seth Warner May 1775 Retaken by the English after the defeat of Arnold at Valcour Island October 1776 Came under American control after surrender of Burgoyne October 1777."

Elaine was growing restive. "Shouldn't we go on," she asked sweetly, "if we're going to have any time to spend at Ticonderoga?"

I'll hurry, Kit planned, and get back to the car first to take the middle seat. But though she walked ahead, somehow or other Elaine managed to get into the car first again and appropriated the place next to Bates.

They approached the fort through a park, stopping to read, sometimes in French and sometimes in English, the tablets which marked the scene of battles or other historic events.

Kit read: "Near this spot stood Louis Joseph de Gozon, Marquis de Montcalm on the 8th of July 1758 with a small force of French troops and Canadian volunteers. He prevented the capture of Fort Carillon by defeating a much superior British force and Colonial army under General Abercrombie."

"This," Kit finished, "is news to me. If anyone had asked me who Louis Joseph de Gozon was, I would never have guessed Montcalm."

Finally they drew up to the fortress, sprawling star-shaped on a promontory jutting out into the lake. "Ticonderoga," read the tablet, "Northern Gateway to the American Colonies." There followed the important dates: Champlain—Iroquois 1609 Montcalm—Abercrombie 1758 Amherst—Bourlamaque 1759 Ethan Allen—De la Place 1775.

In his deep, resonant voice, Bates read the verses underneath, beginning, "Lulled are the passion and the pain, The legend and the race remain," and ending, "And here were men co-equal with their fate, Who did great things, Unconscious they were great."

Of course, Kit agreed, they had probably done what they felt it was their duty to do, with no consciousness of making history.

They went through the sally port, leading from the inner

to the outer works and came out on the west demilune. They walked about the wide, stone-walled terrace. Elaine was interested in looking down at the site of the old French village which had huddled under the protection of the guns of the fort and she even enjoyed the magnificent view southward down the lake. Certainly no enemy ship could have sailed unscathed past these cannon, Kit thought, and viewing the whole great edifice, with its inner and outer defenses bristling with guns, she could not imagine how foot soldiers of colonial times, even with the help of artillery, could ever have taken it. In 1758, she read without surprise, a force of 3,000 French regulars and Canadian volunteers had withstood the attack of 10,000 British Regulars and 5,000 Colonials, when the famous 42nd Highlanders, nicknamed the Black Watch, had sustained such heavy losses.

When they could at last tear Bates away from the old cannon which thrust their polished noses through the thick stone walls at regular intervals, they went through the passageway to the Place d'Armes. Kit read the plaque, "Through this entrance to the Place d'Armes of this fort have passed George Washington, Benjamin Franklin, Benedict Arnold, Horatio Gates, Anthony Wayne, Arthur St. Clair, Henry Knox, Philip Schuyler, and a host of other great men of American history. You who tread in their footsteps, remember their glory."

In the heavy, iron-studded garrison gate, they saw the "wicket," a small door in the gate itself, which was open on May 10, 1775 when Ethan Allen, Benedict Arnold, and eighty-two Green Mountain boys, having crossed the lake in the teeth of a gale, stole through to the Place d'Armes before the alarm could be given by the dozing sentry and de-

manded the surrender of the fort "in the name of the great
Jehovah and the Continental Congress."

"Although," Bates said with a grin, "I've read he had no
direct commission from either of them."

"Men from Vergennes were probably among those Green
Mountain boys," Kit said dreamily. "I wonder if any of my
ancestors could have been with them."

Her lively imagination filled the big Place d'Armes with
drilling soldiers. She could see the sun flash on lines of mus-
kets and polished boots. She could see the gleam of bright
cockades in tricorn hats and the white trousers and red coats
of the British and the buff and blue of the Colonials, for at
one time or another both must have drilled in this square.
She could not help thrilling at the thought of eighty-four
men capturing this huge strongly fortified place without firing a shot.

After the Revolution, Ticonderoga and other state lands
had been deeded to Columbia College and Union College,
just as the Split Rock range across the lake from the Turners' cottage had been. In 1816 William Ferris Pell had leased
the fort and the farms. Distressed to have such a landmark
of history falling into ruins, with neighboring farmers helping themselves to doors or windows or whatever they could
carry away, he had bought the place in 1825. His great great-
grandson had devoted most of his life to rebuilding and
restoring the great fort. Now the Ticonderoga Association
maintained the Fort and surrounding grounds for the benefit of the public.

Kit peeked into the rooms of the Officer of the Day,
which were set up just as they were when in use, with the
office in front and the austere bedroom beyond. His duties,

exactly as given in the regulation books of the day, were tacked up on the wall. It fired her imagination to walk around the restored fort which, instead of being floorless and roofless like Crown Point, was so nearly as it must have been when redcoats and colonial soldiers guarded its ramparts.

Up in back of Fort Ticonderoga at Fort Mount Hope, they saw the partially rotted hand-hewn timbers and hand-wrought nails of the hull of one of Arnold's ships which had been salvaged from the bottom of the lake.

Kit, stirred by the thought of looking at the very boards that had known the tramp of those brave Americans of a long bygone day, spoke of reading in her grandfather's book of the terror throughout the countryside as the stories spread of the large force the British General Carleton was gathering in Canada, and the gunboats he was building to sweep the colonial forces from the lake.

"Think of having to cut down trees and haul them to the mill in order to build the boats with which to take on part of the British navy!" Bates said. "B. Arnold had quite an assignment. Those early Americans were a dauntless breed."

"They had a terrible time getting equipment—sails, guns, cordage—because it all had to be hauled such long distances into the wilderness," Kit contributed.

"But by August, the indomitable B. Arnold had nine ships ready for action," Bates added. "Can you picture them on a hazy October day sailing up the narrows to take on the seasoned gunboats and well-trained crews of the British? To think that they went past the very shores where we bat our tennis balls!"

"It sure was an uneven fight," Kit agreed. "The hastily

built sloops of the untrained colonials against a slice of the famous British navy with nothing less than control of the whole continent of North America as the prize!"

Bates's eyes met hers appreciatively. "From eleven in the morning until five in the afternoon," he went on, "my friend B. Arnold kept the British occupied. At sunset Carleton retired, thinking he had only to wait for daylight to take possession of the badly battered American navy."

"But your daring friend B. Arnold had a different idea," Kit said. "All my life I've thrilled to my father's stories of Arnold quietly leading his ships single file in the dark and foggy night straight through the British lines. Can you imagine old Carleton's rage and astonishment to find his bird flown? Of course he set off in hot pursuit and I love the story of his firing away with his cannon at a shape in the fog he thought was one of Arnold's boats, only to find he had been wasting his ammunition on the rocky island we call Carleton's Prize or Sloop Island. Many times in fog or haze it has looked to me so exactly like a sloop looming up out of the mist, that I can easily understand how the General made his mistake."

Elaine had been out of the conversation quite long enough. Now she asked, "What happened to your friend, B. Arnold, Bates?"

"He stopped at Schuyler's Island to repair his battered boats," Bates answered, "and continued his retreat. He sent the main part of his fleet to safety at Ticonderoga. With his flagship, *Congress,* and a few other vessels he fought a rearguard action with the pursuing British. Just off Split Rock —you know that point on the opposite shore just north of us—Carleton caught up with him and a running battle took place which lasted twenty-one hours."

"How would you like to have been a pioneer wife," Kit asked, "with your ears deafened by the constant echo of the cannonading from the Palisades, while you waited through all those long hours in desperate anxiety for the outcome of the battle which could very well mean an attack on your home?"

"She'll have a chance to think about that," Bates said. "Elaine will make a perfect terrified pioneer wife for one of our tableaux."

Kit felt a nasty pang of jealousy, but she reminded herself that she had expected this and took up the story of the naval battle. "At last Arnold saw that escape was impossible, so he ran his boats ashore and burned them with flags flying. He and his men escaped to Crown Point. The American navy had been momentarily wiped out, but the lake had been saved for another year for before the British could launch another offensive, winter had set in and the lake was closed to navigation."

"I can't understand how a guy like that could later have turned traitor," Bates said in honest puzzlement.

"Most history books make everything in the past seem so simple and clear cut," Kit mused. "Our famous men always seem to have had no trouble at all in coming up with all the right answers. It's so easy looking back from here to see clearly the right and the wrong. But really I suppose there must have been the same argument and confusion then about loyalty to the king or the right to freedom and independence as we have now over the right way to deal with communists at home and abroad, the farm problems, our allies, one mess in the Far East and another in the Middle East . . ." She made a little grimace and gestured with her hands in hopeless bewilderment.

Elaine had had enough history for one day. "Haven't we seen enough?" she asked plaintively. "Can't we have lunch now? I'm starving."

It was late in the afternoon when Bates dropped Elaine at the Lesters' back door. Kit could see that she was tired after a long and—probably to Elaine—a sometimes boring day, but she smiled sweetly and thanked Bates as if she had had the time of her life.

Kit had just said good-by to Bates at her back door and was watching him drive away when her mother called from the living room.

"Did you have a good time, Kit? Come in. You must be tired." Her voice sounded excited.

Kit hurried in to give her a hug. "What's happened, Mother? You sound as if you had a secret—a pleasant one."

Mrs. Turner laughed. "Oh, Kit, it's such good news. Your father called to tell me that everything is all set for a two-week vacation beginning Friday night. If it's really all right with you and Ken and Aunt Charlotte, we're going to go off by ourselves for a junket through Canada."

Kit suppressed a qualm compounded of envy, lonesomeness at the thought of her mother's absence, and worry over being left with Aunt Charlotte, and said gaily, "How wonderful, Mom! When will you leave—Saturday morning?"

"No, I think I'll let your father have a day to catch his breath. We'll start Sunday morning right after church. Oh,

Kit, keep your fingers crossed that nothing happens this time."

Kit held up both hands with fingers crossed.

"I hope that's Ken," Mrs. Turner said, as they heard a car turn into the driveway. "Mrs. Phoebe has built another nest on the front porch, this time just over the spot where we like to sit in the evenings. I want Ken to take it down before dinner."

"We ought to be complimented that Mrs. Phoebe is so attracted to us," Kit said. "You'd think she'd be afraid to hatch her babies within arm's length of a bunch of humans, especially a hard-hearted woman like you."

"Not Mrs. Phoebe," Mrs. Turner said with feeling, as she walked over to the back door to meet Ken and tell him about that lady's latest. "She has all outdoors to build a nest in, but she's so stubborn there's no room in her small body for anything so weak as fear."

"Here we go again," Ken said, as he walked through the living room, followed by his mother. "Watch it, Mrs. Phoebe, here we come!"

Kit went out on the porch with them. She was glad Mrs. Phoebe was not in her nest at the moment. She felt a wave of sympathy for that intrepid female when she should return to find her second home in a few days demolished.

Ken stepped on the chair his mother was steadying for him. Just as he reached up to dislodge the nest, he lost his balance. Mrs. Turner screamed, and Ken came down heavily on his right foot. When he tried to put his weight on it, he let out an involuntary "Ouch!" and hopped over to the glider.

Mrs. Turner was distressed. "It's all my fault," she kept repeating. "I never should have let my eagerness to get rid of Mrs. Phoebe blind me to the danger of your standing on a chair. I don't know what I was thinking of to let you do such a thing."

Kit helped her mother apply cold compresses to Ken's ankle, but by the time they had finished supper the ankle was so swollen and purple that Mrs. Turner called the doctor. He came down from Vergennes, took one look at Ken's foot and said commiseratingly, "You've got a mean sprain there, boy." Very gently he examined the injured ankle. "You've torn a ligament rather badly."

"Keep up the cold compresses tonight," he told Mrs. Turner. "I'll give him something to ease the pain and make him sleep. That ankle's too swollen for me to strap it now, but bring him up tomorrow and I'll fix it up."

"I suppose this means no swimming or tennis for a day or so," Ken asked disconsolately.

Dr. Clarke gave him a pat on the shoulder. "Sorry, boy," he said. "You'll have to keep off that foot for a couple of days at the very least. Keep it up on a hassock and don't put any weight on it."

"There goes my vacation trip," said Mrs. Turner later to Kit, "and it's all my own fault."

"Don't be silly, Mother," Kit consoled her. "Ken will be fine by the weekend, and certainly I'm old enough to take care of him anyway. Everything will be all right."

But secretly she was dismayed at the prospect of a couple of weeks as hostess to Aunt Charlotte, while Ken was laid up with a sprained ankle.

13

Not Such a Fool Dog

Next morning Mrs. Turner took Ken up to Vergennes, and Dr. Clarke strapped his ankle. When they returned, she established Ken on the back porch where he could at least keep an eye on the comings and goings on the road. He sat with the injured foot on a hassock and was as cross as a snapping turtle until Elaine came over to play canasta with him. She wasn't very good at it, and Ken consistently beat her, which seemed to soothe his fury somewhat.

Bates came to offer his condolences just as Mrs. Turner discovered that they were low on drinking water. Bates offered to drive up to town and asked Kit to ride with him. She was wickedly delighted that Elaine, in her role of ministering angel, could not leave Ken.

As they made the turn by the big pine, Kit noticed that the buttercups and devil's-paintbrush had given way now to the orange of daylilies and the deep purple vetch to the pale blue of chicory, tall against the gray fences. In the fields, goldenrod was already showing a faint yellow, and the pale pink of the sumac held a hint of glory to come.

On the way back, as they were passing the Bushey farm, Jim, rumbling along in his tractor over the hayfield by the road, called out, "Hi, Kit! Got some cute puppies up at the barn. Want to see 'em?"

"Oh, let's stop, Bates," Kit begged. "Just a moment, please."

Bates turned in and drove up to the barn. Kit was out of the car as it stopped. Jim left his tractor and came over to them, and Kit introduced Bates.

"Maggie's got three of the cutest pups you'd ever want to see," Jim said. He went into the barn and came out holding three round yellow and white balls of fur, followed by an anxious Maggie, whimpering a little and keeping her long collie nose pressed against his leg.

The middle puppy's little pointed nose was black like his mother's, and his round bright eyes gazed up at Kit in such a knowing way that she lost her heart to him at once. She reached out and took him from Jim, and he snuggled down contentedly in her arms.

"He sure is a cute little fellow," Kit said when she reluctantly handed him back.

"You can have him, Kit, if you like," Jim told her. "I ain't aimin' to keep any of 'em, but I want to be sure they get good homes."

"I wish I could take him," Kit said longingly, rubbing the puppy's ear. He opened his mouth, yawned widely, and ran his eager pink tongue over her hand in a series of rapturous wet dog kisses. "But Mother's strangely difficult about the pet situation."

Elaine had gone, and Ken was reading a book with the air of a martyred saint when Kit got back. After dinner she went upstairs to shampoo her hair, still thinking about the warm, wriggling ball of fur she had held in her arms. When she came downstairs her mother had joined Ken on the back porch. Kit told her about Jim Bushey's offer of a puppy.

"Do we have to go over the whole thing again," Mrs. Turner asked wearily. "You know how I feel about keeping a dog in an apartment."

"But, Mother," Kit protested, unwrapping the towel wound around her head and squeezing some last drops of water from her hair, "lots of dogs are happy in apartments. And Jim says this dog won't grow so very big. He's only part collie, you know."

"Even a part collie would have to be fed, bathed, exercised," Mrs. Turner observed reasonably.

"I'd take all the care of him myself," Kit promised eagerly. "You wouldn't be bothered at all."

"Yes, I know just how it would be," said Mrs. Turner dryly. "With Ken away at Dartmouth and you busy with after-school activities, I'd be left to walk him and probably bathe and feed him as well." Changing the subject with finality, she continued, "George Denton was here this afternoon. He wants Ken and Ray to drive to Hanover with him over the weekend."

"What fun," Kit said enviously. "Are you ever a lucky dog!" she told Ken.

He grinned. "Of course Mom is worried about my ankle, but I can keep it up in the car, and Doc said I could walk on it a little, day after tomorrow."

"I do think Ken could go by Friday without doing any harm to his ankle," Mrs. Turner said, "and it would give him something pleasant and fairly inactive to do. I hate to have him sitting around here with me, missing all the good times."

"I'll take it easy," Ken promised. "You don't have to worry."

"You remember how George Denton put the idea of Dartmouth in Ken's head that very first summer George came to the lake," Mrs. Turner reminisced. "Ever since then, no other college would do for him."

"No wonder," Kit put in, vigorously toweling her hair. "George told us so much about Dartmouth—skiing, hiking, winter carnival and all—that I have always wished I could go to Dartmouth too!"

"It will be so much less strange for Ken when he goes up next fall as a freshman," Mrs. Turner continued, "having been all over the place beforehand with an alumnus."

"Yea-ah," agreed Kit, "and think of the super trip they'll have across the mountains if the weather holds like this. I wish I were going along." She sighed. With Mother and Dad in Canada and Ken in Hanover, she would be alone with Aunt Charlotte for the weekend. She couldn't be selfish enough to make a fuss though, because she felt that Ken deserved a treat to make up for the bad time he had had with his ankle, and she wouldn't for the world stand in the way of the trip she herself had suggested for her parents. So she finished brightly, "Well, have fun. I'll keep the home fires burning."

Mrs. Turner reached out to give Kit's hand a little squeeze. "Kit, darling," she said, "I do appreciate what you are doing in staying at home alone with Aunt Charlotte."

Embarrassed, Kit said, "Think nothing of it." She got up. "My tennis is getting rusty with all this junketing around the country in pursuit of history. I think I'll get in a little practice."

She braided her half-dry, rust-colored hair into two short stiff pigtails which she tied with blue ribbons, picked up her tennis racquet, and went out to bat balls against the side of the house. Except for the pigtails she looked like a young boy in blue pedal pushers and a soft, blue, turtle-neck sweater, borrowed for the moment from Ken.

Colors were brilliant and outlines sharp in the atmosphere of the late afternoon. The wooded hills on the opposite shore were a bright green, and the narrow strip of sandy beach stood out clear and white. Beyond the tawny gold of the back meadows Kit could see the deep blue masses of the Green Mountains, and to the left, across the tumbling white-caps of the lake, range upon range of the Adirondacks mounted in splashes of periwinkle, lavender, and gray against the deep blue of the sky.

Running back to retrieve a ball, Kit saw Bates and Elaine coming down the road. She slammed up on the back porch, flinging her racquet on the table and herself on the nearest chair.

"Here comes Bates with the lily maid," she burst out in disgust, "and she's got 'precious 'ittle doggums' with her. I could see his yellow bow."

"I don't know why you feel the way you do about Elaine," Mrs. Turner said, with the patient resignation of frequent repetition. "She's really a very sweet girl, and it wouldn't hurt you to acquire a few of her womanly qualities."

"Heaven forbid that I should ever languish like the lily maid," declared Kit with feeling.

She watched the couple drawing nearer, Bates limping along in the ruts of the dirt road and Elaine walking carefully beside him. She saw them wave, as the bellowing of

"Old MacDonald Had a Farm" rose above the hum of an approaching automobile. The car stopped, picked up Bates and Elaine, and drove up to the Turners' back porch on a lusty "Eee—" Four doors opening simultaneously, and George Denton, Ray, Bud, and Bates squabbled good-naturedly for the honor of helping Elaine from the car. Kit was amused to see Ken pick up "precious 'ittle doggums" when he came sniffing around his chair, though Ken had always referred to the animal as "that fool dog of Elaine's."

"We're all set," George called out, "to leave for Dartmouth Friday."

"You're making off with an important part of my cast," Bates said ruefully, "and nobody seems to care very much."

"Sorry, old man," George said pleasantly. "But I'll have them back safe and sound next week, when I understand you will have the thing whipped into shape and ready for rehearsals."

"What shall I bring you, Brick Top," Ray Tabor asked, tweaking one of Kit's braids, "as a token of my affection and a memento of the college of my choice?"

"A picture of Eleazer Wheelock," Kit answered at once, naming the founder of Dartmouth who, so the song has it, went into the wilderness to convert the Indians and took along five hundred gallons of good New England rum.

"Let's go inside," Mrs. Turner suggested. "It's cold out here, now that the sun has gone. Come, Ken, I'll help you."

"Nonsense, Mother," Ken said, half amused, half annoyed at her solicitude. "I can get into the living room under my own steam."

One end of the big room, which ran across the front of the whole house and served as living and dining room, was filled with a huge fireplace, around which were grouped a sofa, a coffee table and several chintz-covered easy chairs.

"Since Ken is *hors de combat,* would you please put another log on the fire for me, Ray?" Mrs. Turner asked.

Elaine dropped gracefully down on a fat hassock, where the firelight played on her bright curls. Kit had to admit that she looked very pretty in her yellow dress, cuddling the tawny Pekingese.

"What do you think?" Elaine demanded in her high, little-girl voice. "We're going away, too. Uncle Jim Lester's going to drive Mother and me to Quebec to-morrow morning. I'm just dying to see it and have a chance to practice my French."

"Better watch out for those Frenchies, Gorgeous," Bud said. "They go for beautiful blondes like you."

Elaine giggled. "You silly boy," she simpered. "What chance has a pale little blonde like me among all those colorful French-Canadian girls?" She beamed around the circle, waiting for their reassurance which, Kit noticed, was quickly forthcoming from all the boys together.

"It's awful for us to run off like this one after another," Elaine said, smiling penitently up at Bates where he stood by the fire. "But I've promised Bates I'll put in some extra rehearsals after we all get back."

"Why couldn't you get together and all be away at the same time?" Bates asked. "That wouldn't be quite so hard on the poor producer."

"I have to go when Uncle Jim asks me," Elaine protested. "But here's the cruel, sad part. Uncle Jim, the old tyrant, says I simply can not take my precious 'ittle doggums with me, and my heart's just about broken."

Kit groaned inwardly, as Ken murmured, "Gee, Elaine, that's tough." Faker, she thought. If Elaine only knew what he really thinks of "precious 'ittle doggums."

"I didn't know what to do," Elaine went on in pretty helplessness, and then—she turned appealingly to Mrs. Turner and Kit— "I thought maybe you would keep him for me, Kit; that is, if your Mother doesn't mind."

Kit was shocked. She wanted a dog all right, but a regular he-man beast—not a pampered lap dog.

In stunned silence she heard her Mother say, "Why, of course, Elaine dear. I'm sure Kit would love to take care of Ah-Ting for you. She was teasing for a dog only this afternoon."

Ken—the traitor—echoed, "Sure thing, Elaine; Kit will be glad to take care of him. You won't have to worry. Kit's great with animals."

Desperately Kit babbled, "Oh, no, Elaine! Really I couldn't. I wouldn't dare take the responsibility. He might get sick or run away or die or something, and think how awful you'd feel. I simply couldn't do it."

Even Bates said, "Why, Kit, I'm surprised. I thought you'd enjoy doing it. You seemed so taken with Maggie's puppy this morning."

All the boys were looking at her, Kit thought, as if she were the sort of person who would slap a baby. She glared back at them. Catch any of them allowing himself to be saddled with Ah-Ting!

Mrs. Turner exclaimed, "Why, Kit, how ungracious of you!"

"Come on, Kit, be a sport," Ken urged. "It won't hurt you to take care of the pooch for a few days."

"If you won't do it, Kit," Elaine said plaintively, "Mother and I will just have to stay home. There's no one else I'd trust."

"But of course we will keep him for you," Mrs. Turner assured her. "I don't know what's got into Kit."

Bates joined in, "Much as I hate to lose my star for a week," he said, "I wouldn't want her to miss the trip on account of Ah-Ting. I'll help you with him, Kit. Maybe we can show him some of New England's historic places while his mistress is gone."

Kit could not tell whether he was trying to help her or Elaine. Probably both of us, she told herself; Bates is always kind. But though she hated to admit it even to herself, she was getting a little fed up with the history of Vermont.

Ray murmured into her ear. "Looks like you're stuck with the fool dog, Brick Top."

"Oh, hush up, will you!" Kit snapped.

When the Lesters stopped next day Elaine brought not only her darling, but his sweaters; a transparent, wrap-around garment bound in plaid, which she said was his raincoat; his basket; his pillow and blanket; his brush and comb; his soap and towel; his harness and leash; a variety of ribbon bows, and a box of toys!

"He's just had a bath," she explained, "but I brought his soap and towels in case he should get wet or dirty. Be sure to put on his sweater if he's outdoors when it's cold, or his raincoat if it's raining. He always sleeps in his basket and he's very unhappy if he doesn't have his own blanket and pillow —isn't muvver's precious?"

Kit listened in disgust to the rest of Elaine's minute instructions. When his mistress had finally planted a tearful kiss on Ah-Ting's nose and been whirled away, Kit reached down and removed the dog's harness and bow. "While you're with me," she promised solemnly, "you'll be treated like a regular dog—no bows or baby talk."

A ripple ran over Ah-Ting's back. He gave himself a shake and sat down in front of Kit, studying her gravely with his head tilted a little to one side. "This begins well," his expression seemed to say, "but I'm wary. I've been fooled before." In spite of herself, Kit laughed and leaned down to scratch behind his long, silky ears. "Fool dog," she said, but her voice was kind.

Ah-Ting evidently made up his mind that here was a friend. He backed off a bit and sat up on his hind legs, waving his front paws in the air. Then he came down on all fours, rushed over and jumped on her lap, gazing up at her soulfully out of bulging, round brown eyes.

"Come on, my friend," Kit said, "none of this lap-dog stuff, understand?" She lifted her hand to push him off her lap and felt his soft, wet tongue caressing her fingers.

From that moment Ah-Ting could not bear to let Kit out of his sight. Mrs. Turner, Ken, Aunt Charlotte, Martha, he tolerated with a condescending courtesy, but Kit he adored with every inch of his small, wriggling body. He was determined to stand high in the bow when she paddled her canoe, the wind sweeping his long ears and the plume of his tail. When she went swimming, he plunged in and swam after her, his wet hair plastered smoothly to his skull and his round, pushed-in-nose sticking out of the water.

But worst of all, in spite of what Elaine had said about his being unable to sleep except in his own basket, he insisted on spending the night on the foot of Kit's bed, and he snored long and loud through his pug nose. Kit shut him up with his basket in the kitchen, but he made such a fuss that she let him out and made the best of it. Although she would not have admitted it for anything, she was secretly pleased by the little dog's devotion.

The days were not without their alarms, however. The afternoon after Elaine left, Mrs. Turner and Kit were sitting on the high, unrailed front veranda, almost six feet above the ground. Suddenly a chipmunk streaked across the lawn. Instantly Ah-Ting sprang from the glider and sailed through the air in a wild leap after the insolent rodent which had dared to invade his domain. Kit sprang up in alarm, but the small dog was speeding unhurt after the chattering chipmunk. The little animal scampered up a tall pine tree, scolding and hurling insults down at his pursuer. At first Ah-Ting barked back; then, realizing the futility of competing with the shrill termagant, he settled himself comfortably to wait until the provoking creature should descend.

Kit began to laugh. "Isn't he a fool dog?" she asked her mother. "He certainly gave me a scare, sailing through the air like that!"

Mrs. Turner bent her head over the pink wool in her lap. "Were you afraid he might get hurt?" she questioned dryly.

"Oh, I wasn't concerned so much about Ah-Ting," Kit answered quickly. "I was thinking of Elaine. She'd never forgive me if anything happened to her darling."

Mrs. Turner hid a smile behind her knitting. And that was not the only occasion on which she smiled quietly to herself during the next two days. Ah-Ting's body might be small, but his heart held the courage of a lion. Undaunted by the size of the Summers' lumbering chow, he flew at the great black beast in such a frenzy that the chow, taken aback, loped off for home. Ah-Ting came back in triumph, flaunting his plumed tail high. It was quite evident that he felt entirely capable of guarding the Turner premises against all comers.

He did not fare so well in his skirmish with the milk boy. Johnny Armstrong, riding up with the milk in the basket on his bike, was so startled by the barking bundle of tawny fur that he lost control, and Johnny, bike, and bottles of milk came hurtling down on the dog. Ah-Ting suffered a cut paw, and Mrs. Turner, Ken, Martha, and Aunt Charlotte were quietly amused at Kit's elaborate explanation that she carried the dog upstairs at night and down in the morning only for Elaine's sake.

But the day that Kit, coming up from the lake, screamed as she almost stepped on a small brown toad, and Ah-Ting, rushing to the defense of his beloved, fell upon the creature and killed it—that was the worst of all. Later in the day, the dog was violently sick and rolled over on his back. Kit picked him up and carried him to the kitchen. When she put him down his body was rigid, his paws sticking out stiffly, and he was panting desperately.

"Land's sake!" Martha exclaimed, in her soft singing voice. "What ails him? Is he dyin', Kit?"

"I don't know," Kit quavered. "He killed a toad. I think that or something else he got hold of in the woods has been too much for his stomach to take."

She knelt and stroked the dog's head, with a shaking hand murmuring soothing endearments that, she would have been ashamed to realize, rivaled Elaine's.

Ah-Ting whimpered a little, looking up at Kit beseechingly with glazed eyes. His nose was hot and dry against her hand. He tried feebly to lick her wrist, but could not quite make it, and the plume of his tail, which he usually carried so proudly arched over his back, drooped low.

"What can we do?" Kit asked in desperation. "We can't just let him die! Where's Mother?"

"She and your Aunt Charlotte took Ken up to the doctor's for the last time before he goes off to Hanover tomorrow."

Kit groaned. "No car to take him to the vet."

Ah-Ting whimpered again and his legs twitched convulsively. Kit knelt beside him, and there were tears in her eyes as she looked up at Martha. "If this is caused by that toad, he did it for me, Martha," she explained. "He thought he was protecting me. I can't bear it if he dies."

There was now no pretense that she was worried only for Elaine's sake. "Oh, Martha," she wailed, "what shall I do?"

"Don't fret so," Martha's soft voice encouraged. "We'll just make him bring it up, whatever it is, that's all." She moved quickly about the kitchen.

"Let me see now—hot water and mustard. Here you are, Kit—think you can make him swallow this?"

Kit poured some of the liquid between Ah-Ting's teeth and held his mouth until he swallowed. Whimpering, he tried to pull his head away, looking at her reproachfully. Kit's heart contracted. It seemed cruel to force him to take the loathsome concoction, but if Martha thought it would help, she would make him take it, if it killed her.

Presently the dose had its effect, and after the retching paroxysms were over, Ah-Ting lay back weakly against

Kit's knee. His nose was still dry and hot, but he was no longer panting so hard and the terrifying rigidity had gone out of his body.

"I think that did it, Martha," Kit exulted. "I don't think he's going to die."

"My goodness, no!" Martha agreed. "Take a lot to kill that spunky Ah-Ting."

"You were wonderful," Kit said, beaming at Martha. "How did you know what to do?"

"Oh, I've been around young ones a lot," Martha said complacently.

Kit spent most of that night hopping in and out of bed, making sure that Ah-Ting was all right. The little dog was still weak and refused food, but he lapped feebly at the bowl of water Kit held for him.

The next morning she carried him out where the hot sun was drawing spicy scents from a warm bed of pine needles, and by evening she was thankfully watching him chase fireflies across the lawn.

Tomorrow Elaine would come for him. Thank goodness he was all right. Kit hated to admit how much she would miss the fool dog. She whistled from the porch, where she was sitting with her mother, and he came bounding up the steps and jumped into her lap.

In the dimness Mrs. Turner stretched out her hand to her daughter. "I know how much you'll miss the little beggar, Kit," she said. "I must admit you've cared for him faithfully. We'll have to see what we can find to take his place. Maybe Jim Bushey still has one of the puppies he offered you."

14

Summer Storm

Even her mother's change of heart did not cheer Kit next day after Elaine, bubbling over with thanks, had reclaimed Ah-Ting. The little dog had been so constantly at Kit's side for the past few days that she missed him at every turn.

This was to be a season of departures, she thought, and she hated good-bys. Mrs. Turner, trim as usual in one of her favorite tailored white dresses, her short black hair brushed back from her face, her large earrings gleaming white against the deep tan of her skin, was somewhat distractedly running up and down between her room and Ken's, putting things in her own bags and going up to make sure that Ken was doing a proper job with his packing or to urge him to be careful about this or that.

"For Pete's sake, Mom," Ken said at last, "you act like a mother hen in a frenzy, as the duckling she hatched takes to the water. I *won't* forget my pajamas and I *can* manage to stow away the few things I'll need for the weekend. I promise you I won't do anything foolish to set back my ankle, because I want to get in some more tennis and water skiing before the summer's over. Quit fussing, like a good girl, and let your little boy stand on his own feet, even if one of them is slightly battered."

Mrs. Turner laughed a little ruefully. "I suppose I am silly," she conceded, "but I can't help feeling that all the pain and discomfort of your ankle was my fault, and I don't want anything to spoil this trip for you, if I can help it. I'll go down now and get along with my own packing."

The boys left before noon. Kit experienced a lonely, left-behind feeling that was only partly alleviated by the thought of working with Bates on the pageant.

Next morning Kit accompanied her parents to St. Paul's Episcopal Church in Vergennes, which her four or five times great-grandfather had been instrumental in founding. The handsome young rector took as his text, ". . . whosoever shall say [to his brother] Thou fool, shall be in danger of hell fire," and Kit couldn't help feeling that somehow his sermon had a special meaning for her.

Kit knew that he used the word brother in its broadest sense and she began to have a lively sense of guilt about her feeling for Elaine. When the time came to approach the altar to receive communion she was in a thoroughly contrite mood. She knelt at the rail beside her mother with eyes repentantly downcast. She raised them for a moment just as Father Hopkins lifted the chalice from her mother's lips and moved toward her. A shaft of sunlight played on the golden cup and struck sparks from the jewels with which it was encrusted.

Kit had taken communion from it before, but never had she seen it sparkling like this in sunshine. Over a hundred years ago the congregation of this small church had been moved to acquire fitting vessels for the communion service.

They had sent their gold and silver and their jewels to Scotland, and there this beautiful chalice had been made. Kit had heard her father say that when it first came from Scotland, it was the second most beautiful communion cup in the whole country. It thrilled Kit to know it was not the gift of one wealthy parishioner, but the loving generosity of many people who had been willing to give up their jewels to adorn it—pearls, diamonds, rubies, amethysts, sapphires, and some very lovely coral.

Kit had seen the box of polished oak in which it was kept. With hand-wrought brass lock and hinges, it had been lovingly fashioned of "Arnold's Oak," a beam from one of Benedict's ships.

After the service, Kit and Aunt Charlotte said good-by to Mr. and Mrs. Turner, with many last-minute admonitions to be careful, not to worry about them, and to have fun. She and Aunt Charlotte drove back to the lake with the Lesters.

They were on their own now, Kit thought, and, with no power boat and no car, pretty much confined to the cottage until Ken's return. She couldn't go off all day with what was left of the young crowd and leave Aunt Charlotte to her own lonely devices. Naturally Aunt Charlotte didn't play tennis or water ski. She didn't go swimming, as Mrs. Turner did even on the coldest days. What in the world could Kit do to entertain her?

Martha served them a delicious dinner, but the table looked strange and lonely with only the two places. After the dishes were done, Martha too went off for the rest of the day with a nephew who came for her in his car. Supper would be Kit's business. She wasn't looking forward to it, especially under Aunt Charlotte's critical inspection, but she

hoped she could open a can and heat up some soup, or make
a few sandwiches and a pot of coffee that would pass mus-
ter.

When Aunt Charlotte went up to her room for a nap, Kit
sat in the glider on the front porch with her grandfather's
history book, which Bates had returned yesterday. He had
worked hard on the script for the last few days and was
ready to write into it a scene about Macdonough and the
Battle of Plattsburg.

Mr. Turner had told Kit before he left that if the pageant
was well in hand—scenes set, parts assigned, script in shape
for him to read when he came back from Canada—he
would get busy on promoting the performance. He had
planned articles for the local papers, posters for store windows and other strategic spots, handbills, billboards, and a
couple of radio features on local stations where he knew the
managers.

While Aunt Charlotte was napping, Kit planned to catch
up with Bates on Macdonough, the Battle of Plattsburg, and
the War of 1812 as it touched Lake Champlain. Maybe Bates
might want to drive over to Plattsburg tomorrow and
would invite Aunt Charlotte to come along. That would be
something for her to do.

So engrossed was Kit that she was unaware of the great,
dark thunderheads piling up above the hills on the opposite
shore, until a jagged fork of lightning cut through the
black sky, and the echo of distant thunder rumbled from the
Palisades.

Kit dropped her book and jumped to her feet. We're in
for it, all right, she thought, as she ran down the stone steps
to the dock. Storms from the northwest, rarely by-passing

this strip of eastern shore, almost invariably wreaked here the full force of their fury. Kit knew that much had to be done in order to ride out such storms with as little damage as possible.

She dragged the canoes out of the water and struggled valiantly to get them to the security of a sheltered spot under an overhanging ledge of rock. She made the skiff and flat-bottomed rowboat fast with extra ropes from bows to dock and sterns to trees on shore. She threw out the storm anchor of the *Kittyken* and checked her bow and stern moorings.

When she had done all she could to protect the boats, she ran back to the house. The wind was already crashing through the trees and whipping the lake into a churning mass of giant, spray-topped rollers. Incessantly now the eerie, almost nightlike blackness was split by brilliant flashes of greenish light that illumined the wild scene momentarily with the unnatural brightness of giant klieg lights.

Kit was stripping the porch chairs and glider of their cushions and standing them against the wall when Aunt Charlotte in her dressing gown appeared in the doorway. Aunt Charlotte's serene poise had crumbled. She was wringing her hands, and her eyes were wild with terror. "Katharine!" she screamed above the storm, in a voice shrill with fright. "Come in out of this terrible storm!"

"It's all right, Aunt Charlotte," Kit soothed. "I'm coming in as soon as I fix up the porch. Are the windows all closed?"

"I don't know," Aunt Charlotte moaned. "I'm so frightened. I never saw such a storm. And you and I all alone here—what will we do?"

"We'll be all right," Kit assured her again, as she upended

the last chair, swept the books and magazines off the table, and joined Aunt Charlotte in the living room.

Outside the pandemonium increased in fury. Almost constantly the crash of thunder echoed and re-echoed from the Palisades, and now and then there was the sharp crack of a breaking limb as the old trees were battered by the gale.

Kit ran around upstairs and down, closing windows and doors. Now and then the lights flickered and Aunt Charlotte groaned in terror, and Kit thought they would be left in darkness, but each time they came on again.

Then the rain began, battering the tin roof over the gables, streaming down the windows, spattering down the chimney into the fireplace. After a time a thin trickle of water began to seep under the doors from the front porch and increased until quite a flood was pouring into the room. Kit got the mop from the kitchen and kept sopping it up.

The crashes of thunder seemed almost to coincide with the lightning now. Aunt Charlotte was sobbing in hysterical fright. Kit, busy with her mopping, kept up a steady murmur of reassurance and encouragement. And then it seemed as if a ball of blinding fire exploded with a deafening crash right there in the living room, while rumbling thunder continued to shake the very ground and echoed awesomely from the Palisades. The lights flickered and went out, and this time they did not come back on again.

Kit groped through the darkness for the candles kept for such emergencies in a drawer of the sideboard, found them and lighted two for the silver candlesticks on the dining table and two for the old pewter candlesticks on the mantel over the fireplace.

"That one was right over our heads, so we've probably had

the worst of it," she said brightly to Aunt Charlotte. "The storm will go on up the mountains, so there's nothing to be afraid of now."

But even after the thunder had grown faint in the distance and the rain had stopped, Aunt Charlotte continued to gasp and tremble. Kit was worried about her. Perhaps a cup of hot tea would quiet her, and it was almost suppertime anyway.

The storm had not cleared the atmosphere, and a warm, sticky twilight was descending. Taking a candle from the table, Kit went out to the kitchen. She was glad they used bottled gas and did not depend on electricity for cooking. No telling when the current would come on again.

While she waited for the water to boil, she was free for the first time to think about the amazing way in which Aunt Charlotte's serenity and assurance had cracked under the strain of the storm, so that she had suddenly become as helpless and terrified as a child. It's not the years alone that bring maturity, Kit thought, in a flash of insight as illuminating as the lightning. In the momentary glow of this realization, she saw clearly how silly it was to yearn to be grown up, expecting that suddenly when one had turned sixteen, say—or eighteen—one would be transformed in one magic moment into a serene and confident individual who knew all the answers. She was beginning to understand dimly that one acquired this sort of maturity slowly, a little here and a bit there, and went on acquiring it all through life. At any time, at any age, one might find oneself unsure of the right answer or be helpless in a strange situation.

Kit made sandwiches, cut two pieces of the cake Martha had left and piled them with the hot tea on the big black

flower-decorated tray. She and Aunt Charlotte had supper companionably before the fire by candlelight. Later when they were going up to bed, each with a candle to light her way, Kit kissed Aunt Charlotte with real affection, knowing she would never again feel in awe of her great-aunt.

15

In Charge of Aunt Charlotte

The boys returned early Monday evening. They had had a marvelous time and were full of enthusiasm for Dartmouth. It was some time before Ray Tabor had a chance to talk to Kit alone.

"Come out to the car a minute, Brick Top," he invited. "I have your present for you."

"Why didn't you bring it in?" Kit demanded. "Ray Tabor, tell me this instant what it is!"

"Not so fast," he teased, catching her by the arm, and walking with maddening slowness toward the car. "You know," he said, turning her to face him and taking her in, from the wreath of blue flowers around the soft bun into which she had twisted her curls to the blue dress and the trim white sandals, "I didn't see a single view in the whole state of New Hampshire to compare with what I'm looking at right now."

"Why, Ray!" Kit stammered in pleased confusion. Then she began to pull him toward the car. "Come on," she urged. "The present! I'm just dying of curiosity."

He opened the back door, reached into a box on the

floor of the car, and held up a wriggling wire-haired terrier puppy, with one white ear cocked perkily upright and one black one flopped over his eye.

Kit gave a squeal and made a dive for the puppy. "The darling!" she cried. "The adorable darling! Oh, Ray, is he really for me?"

"Nobody else, Brick Top," Ray said, pleased with her enthusiasm. "I figured that just about now you'd be missing Ah-Ting, fool dog though he is, and this piece of no-good baggage—he's already chewed up my shoelaces— would cheer you up. That is, if your mother will let you keep him."

"He's a darling," said Kit, "and from something Mother said before she left I know she'll let me keep him. But, Ray," she objected, loyal to Ah-Ting's devotion, "Elaine's pet isn't such a fool dog as she makes you think. She's the foolish one. Ah-Ting is really a nice dog. We had a wonderful time together."

Ray laughed. "That's the way I had it figured out when I bought his nibs here!"

His Nibs, as they had immediately begun to call the puppy, took Ah-Ting's place at the foot of Kit's bed. He whimpered once or twice during the night, but most of the time he was, as Kit said, "a perfect lamb."

The terrible storm had not cleared the atmosphere. It was even hotter and stickier than ever. "We won't have clear weather," Kit told Aunt Charlotte, "until the wind changes and blows from the north."

Up beyond the Armstrong farm, men were working on the power and telephone lines. The Kimballs' dock section of the lake shore was still without telephone or electricity. Martha's nephew had brought a big cake of ice from town, and they had stored the perishables in the huge old built-in icebox of Kit's grandfather's day. They had to depend on kerosene lamps and candles after dark in the welcome pine-scented coolness, and so they had been going to bed shortly after the lovely peach and saffron afterglow faded behind the black mass of the Adirondacks. Kit was afraid Aunt Charlotte was bored and probably wishing herself back in Virginia. She was busy at the moment straightening her room, washing her personal things, and saying her prayers. All of which occupied her for an hour or so every day.

Kit was slumped lazily on the dock, swinging her legs back and forth above the water. Leaning down she could see a school of perch flashing where the sun slanted through the clear depths. If she only had her fishing rod—but it was too hot to go up to the house for it. And if she did go, there wouldn't be any fish by the time she came back, anyway.

She swung around a bit to look at the *Kittyken,* moored securely between the ell of the dock and the shore, and was aware of the hum of a motor vibrating across the water. A small boat was heading diagonally across the lake from Barn Rock Harbor. Before she could distinguish its occupants, Kit knew it was Bates Cunningham and Ray Tabor coming back from a swim in the bottomless, icy water at the foot of the old abandoned ore mine. She swallowed a very un-Kit-like flutter in her throat and wished she had changed into her new green Bermudas. But Bates only raised an arm in greeting, while Ray sang out, "Hi, Brick Top," as he cut across the bay.

A flash of pink on the Lester dock caught Kit's eye.

"Elaine, the lily maid," she thought grimly. Even at this distance, by the way the wind fluttered Elaine's dress, Kit could imagine how crisp and unwrinkled it was. She thought she could see spotless white shoes flash in the sun, and she pictured carefully arranged gold curls and a daintily powdered nose. She glanced ruefully down at her own dirty sneakers, and navy shorts, rumpled from a set of tennis.

The sound of the motor died on the still air. Kit could see the boys' boat floating idly in front of the Lesters' dock.

"We're going to Westport," Ray shouted. "If you want to look for that material Bates says you need for your costume, come on along."

Elaine's reply came clearly across the water. "Oh, Ray darling, you're perfectly sweet to ask me, and I'd just love to go, but I promised . . ."

Kit gave a final disgusted slam of her sneakers against the dock, rose, and trudged up to the house. She could sit around miserably, grubbing through her grandfather's books to supply Bates with material for his old plays; she could knock herself out as Ray's partner in a tennis tournament; but when it came to dances and parties and boat rides, they both, as usual, rushed to invite Elaine. At the back of her mind she knew she was being unfair, but she took a perverse sort of pleasure in making herself unhappy. With her stupid self-consciousness, her sunburned face, pale brows and lashes, she just wasn't attractive to boys. She might as well go in for sports and be a sort of spinster Babe Zaharias, for she knew she would never marry. It would help to be famous, though, and she'd better give up wasting her time on stupid history books that really bored her and get on with tennis, water skiing, diving, and swimming—at least she had some chance there.

But, however much unwanted, Bates's thin face, with his shadowed blue eyes smiling, floated before her, and she could hear the thrilling music of his deep voice. Her breath caught in her throat. "Bates, Bates," she cried under her breath, as she walked up to the house. "I wish I'd never seen you."

Delectable odors of baking came from the kitchen, where Martha, for all her two hundred pounds, was stepping lightly about. She had just opened the oven door on a pan of golden-brown cookies when Kit came in. The sight of the cookies considerably comforted her broken heart.

"Y—u—m—m," she said, wrinkling her nose to sniff. "They smell divine. Give, Martha, give."

"For the land's sakes, Kit," Martha said in her slow drawl, "can't you let the cookies even get cool before you come around with your mouth waterin'? A body can't get nothin' laid by in this house without you or Ken comes along and gobbles it up."

But even as she grumbled, she was dumping four or five of the still-warm cookies on a plate. Kit swooped them up in both hands and went out on the porch. Boy, it was hot! Her heavy, bronze hair, curling around her face and hanging on her shoulders, seemed unbearable, and she twisted it up in a knot on top of her head.

Lying flat on the glider and munching cookies, she fell to dreaming. If she could only run the *Kittyken,* she would take Bates down the river and show him the dug-out. Legend had it that during the Lake Champlain Naval War of 1812 the British thought they had Commander Macdonough and the American ships which he had built in Vergennes penned up in the river, but the ingenious Americans, through information relayed from Fort Cassin at the mouth of the river, dug a channel connecting the river with the bay and sneaked through at night to surprise the enemy. The Americans had fired, demolishing one battleship, and the British had turned and fled. Kit had been through the dug-out with Ken, but it was gradually filling up and she thought that in years to come people would hardly be able to find it.

If she could only point out all these things to Bates and give him sufficient assistance with his play or pageant or whatever it was, he might invite her to be his date at the party his parents were giving for the cast after the performance. She would pile her hair up on top of her head, wear the aqua dress. Bates would see how grown up and sophisticated she really was, and he would . . .

The squeak of the screen door being quietly opened and closed aroused her from her dream. Elaine, with a bowl in her hand, was standing in front of her, laughing. "So the heat's got even you," she said. "I never thought I'd find Kit Turner dreaming in a glider in the middle of the afternoon. I came over to borrow some eggs," she went on. "Bates is coming to dinner, and I'm making a cake, but we forgot to get eggs in town, and it's too hot to walk up to the farm."

Kit could picture the beautiful cake Elaine would make and the smile in Bates's eyes as he complimented her. Elaine has all the other boys dancing attendance, Kit thought; couldn't she leave Bates for me?

Suddenly from within the house came a series of loud thuds, followed by a shrill scream. Kit, with Elaine trailing after her, streaked for the door. Martha was kneeling beside Aunt Charlotte, who was lying doubled up on the little platform at the foot of the dark, narrow stairs. Aunt Charlotte's face was gray-white and her eyes were closed. Kit rushed to her side. "What happened?" she gasped.

"Your aunt must have missed her footin' at the top of the stairs," Martha said, "and plunged down the whole flight. She hit her head on the wall at the bottom and I'm afraid she's hurt bad."

Kit bent over to look and was furious with herself for feeling sick at the sight of the blood staining Aunt Charlotte's white hair and dropping into a little pool on the floor.

"Get me the smelling salts and that bottle of spirits of ammonia from your mother's bedroom, Kit," Martha ordered, "and bring the scissors, some iodine and a bandage."

Kit, with Elaine still trailing ineffectually after her, brought the required articles, and then stood with her stomach doing cartwheels while Martha cut away Aunt Charlotte's matted hair and bathed the deep cut.

"What an idiot I am," she scolded herself. "Turning faint at the sight of a little blood. No wonder Dad won't trust me with the *Kittyken*. He's right. A lot of good I am in an emergency."

As she worked with gentle fingers, Martha looked up at Kit. "Goodness, child," she said, "you're white as chalk. Go get a drink of water. Elaine, stop that moanin' and hand me that bandage. It was a rusty nail that made the cut on Mrs. Penfield's head, and she ought to have an injection right off. My nephew ran a rusty nail in his hand, and the doctor said he didn't have any trouble because he had the injections so quick."

While she talked, Martha was moving the uncorked bottle of smelling salts back and forth under Aunt Charlotte's nose.

"Get Ken to bring the car," Elaine called to Kit.

"Ken's not here," Martha said calmly. "He went over to ride that Morgan horse of Bud Summers'."

"And mother's gone to town," Elaine said. She began to wring her hands. "Oh, what'll we do? All the telephones are still out after that terrible storm. Bates and Ray went to Westport. There's no one to go for help! What'll we do?"

"Dr. Gardner, across the lake at Westport, is a good doctor," Kit said slowly.

"Look," Elaine whispered. "She's coming to."

Aunt Charlotte's eyelashes trembled and she moaned a little. Then her eyelids opened wide and she was looking at them with dull, pain-clouded eyes. After a moment or two when she understood what had happened, she tried to get up from her uncomfortable position, twisted into a ball on the little square of the landing. Martha and Kit helped her to the sofa. She was able to walk the few steps, so they knew her legs were uninjured, but she continued to moan and presently lapsed again into unconsciousness.

"She ought to see a doctor right away," Martha repeated.

Kit considered. Could she take the *Kittyken* safely across the lake? True, it was calm as a Quaker meeting at the moment, and there hadn't been a whiff of breeze all morning, but what if a sudden storm should come up? The thought of being caught in the middle of the lake by such a tempest as they had experienced last Sunday made her quail.

Did she dare disobey her father? If she did, it might be a very long time before he would allow her any of Ken's privileges.

She said aloud, "I—I think I could run across to Westport and get Dr. Gardner." She turned to meet Martha's anxious eyes. "What do you think? Do you think I ought to try it?"

16

"The Wind She Blow"

"You can run that boat every bit as good as Ken," Martha told Kit decisively. "Mrs. Penfield ought to have a doctor right away, and there's no tellin' when Ken or Mrs. Lester'll be home. You'd only waste time runnin' up and down the lake shore tryin' to find somebody to go for a doctor. You go on over to Westport, Kit, and fetch Dr. Gardner, but you be mighty careful, child."

"Kit, you wouldn't!" Elaine stopped whimpering in surprise. "They've never found bottom in some places on the other side. You wouldn't dare go over all alone. What would your father say?"

"I don't know," Kit snapped nervously, "and I don't care. We can't just leave Aunt Charlotte to die of a fractured skull or get lockjaw from that rusty nail. I know I can manage the *Kittyken* and I'm going to do it."

Kit ran out of the house and down the steps. She scrambled under the porch to pull out the oars, and, one in each hand, she banged them step by step down the stone stairs to the dock. I hope I don't have to use them, she thought with a pang of misgiving.

Streams of perspiration trickled down her back, and her face was flushed and damp from her efforts. The big red can of gasoline and the sticky old quart bottle Ken used for oil were in the pump house. Kit collected them, the life preservers, and the fire extinguisher, and jumped down into the *Kittyken*.

The outlines of the mountains were vague and misty in the haze. The brooding quiet warned of a storm, or one of those wild blows shrieking out of the north. "I hope I get across before whatever is coming gets here," Kit thought uneasily.

"Wait, Kit!" Elaine was running down the steps. "Wait for me. I'm going with you."

"No, you're not!" Kit shot back quickly. "I'm not going to risk a passenger."

"I'm not going to let you go all alone," Elaine said stubbornly, and before Kit could prevent her she jumped down into the boat.

"Look here, Elaine," Kit protested. "I appreciate your courage and your good intention, but I'd much rather not risk anyone else's neck but my own. Thanks a million, but please get out. You're only making it harder for me."

Elaine settled herself more firmly on the broad stern seat. "I'm going with you and nothing's going to stop me, so you might as well get going. We're losing time when every second counts."

It was true. The hot hushed quiet, the smooth polished-steel look of the water, the limp stillness of the usually dancing birch leaves told Kit that the storm, or whatever it was, was not far off. With set lips, she untied the mooring lines and pushed off from the dock. As she touched the starter she addressed the engine in Ken's favorite terms. "Come on,

Little Eva, be a good girl now. Come on, Little Eva, sweetheart."

And Little Eva came on. On the second try, the engine sputtered and caught. Kit stepped up the speed, shifted gears, and headed across the lake.

The bow of the *Kittyken* cut sharply through the still water. The little breeze caused by their motion was hot on their faces. Kit regretted that she had forgotten a hat. Her nose would be a pretty sight by the time they reached Westport.

Above the noise of the engine, Elaine shouted, "I hope we're doing the right thing. Your father may be awfully angry."

She had powdered her nose, Kit noticed, and looked as fresh and pretty as ever. She patted her perspiring upper lip daintily now with an immaculate white handkerchief. Then she turned to Kit with a worried expression in her chinablue eyes. "Funny looking sky," she said. "Such a queer greenish-yellow. Look at those clouds over there."

Kit's heart gave a little jump. The clouds did have a sinister look, spreading greenish-gray over the horizon. They were out in the broad lake now. Would they make it before the storm broke? Looking back at the drooping flag in front of the Lester place on the rapidly receding shore, she estimated that they had come about a third of the distance.

Suddenly the glassy surface of the lake splintered into tiny ripples. Elaine caught at her yellow scarf as a sudden gust of wind swirled it about her head. Kit's hair, which had been loosely knotted on top of her head, streamed out on the rising wind. It began to pick up strength, shrieking out of the north, and instinctively Kit headed into it.

Soon white caps topped the tumbling waves, then were lost in rushing walls of dark green water. Elaine gave a startled cry when the first icy shower drenched her. The noise of the motor was silenced in the roar of wind and water.

Elaine leaned toward Kit, her face so white that even her lips were pale. "Turn back!" she screamed. "Turn back! We'll be drowned!"

She's scared to death, Kit thought, and realized with a throb of fear that Elaine could hardly swim a dozen strokes. She tried to call out to her, but the wind snatched the words out of her mouth. It was almost impossible to breathe against its rushing force. At times Kit could not see the Vermont shore over the great shoulder of water behind her. Sometimes the propeller, lifted completely out of water, spun madly in the air.

Kit felt a moment of panic. In this mad turmoil of wind and water she was alone, running the *Kittyken,* and responsible for the safety of a passenger who could not swim. She was tempted to follow Elaine's advice and turn back. Lines from the poem she had repeated to Bates came to her. "You can't get drown on Lac Champlain, so long you stay on de shore." How good it would be to have her feet solidly on her own dock again! But common sense told her it would be worse than folly to attempt to go about in such a sea. Broadside to these mountains of water they would surely capsize. They must be as far now from the Vermont shore as from the New York side, and anyway, she just didn't dare do anything but keep right on up the lake facing into the wind, taking the waves head on. What else would Ken do, if he were here?

All at once she knew what Ken would do—it was really the only thing to do—and that was to run diagonally up the lake in the teeth of the wind until she was in the lee of Diamond Island, cross just below Split Rock and run down in the lee of the mountains to Westport Harbor.

She steadied her grip on the wheel. She was calm, now that she knew what she was going to do. Gesturing with one hand, she tried to explain to Elaine and motioned to her to keep the life preservers handy. It was hard to hold the wheel steady against the pounding waves. Kit held it with two blistering hands. If only Little Eva kept on turning. If the engine ever died in this sea . . . She found herself repeating over and over through clenched teeth, "Come on, Little Eva! Come on, Little Eva!"

Then, its outline distorted through flying spray, Diamond Island loomed ahead. Kit knew she must be careful here, because of the shifting and uncertain sand bar which ran out from the southern shore. Suddenly she felt the boat steady in the calmer waters as she gained the lee of the island, and she realized she could breathe now without effort. Carefully she slowed for the turn, murmuring prayerful endearments to the engine, and Little Eva responded magnificently with a heart-warming, steady throbbing.

As they ran out from the lee of the island and headed diagonally south before the wind, a great wave broke over the stern, but Kit hardly felt the icy deluge which plastered her shirt and shorts to her body. As a second wave broke, Elaine slid off the seat and crouched, moaning, in the bottom of the boat. With the wind at her back now, Kit could make her passenger hear. She kicked a can down to Elaine and shouted for her to bail. Action seemed to be good for Elaine, and she stopped her hysterical crying as she bailed with desperate energy.

Hot needles of pain ran across Kit's shoulders. Her arms were numb and her hands seemed to burn to the very bone. She felt that it was only the occasional slap of the cold waves breaking over her that kept her from slumping down in the bottom of the boat beside Elaine. Then, through the wet strands of hair blown over her face, she could see the jagged outline of an arm of land sliding by on her right, and maneuvering carefully, she brought the *Kittyken* into the comparative peace of Westport Harbor. Arms trembling with fatigue, she brought the boat alongside the landing in a way that even Ken would have admired.

Elaine scrambled out on the dock on her hands and knees. Kit was shocked by her first good look at her passenger. Elaine's crisp cotton dress, now soaked and bedraggled, dripped on the cement of the dock. Her hair, lank and wet, straggled about her white face.

Coming with me was a wonderfully brave thing for her to do, Kit thought. I'll never forget it. Maybe she can't win a swimming race or a tennis match, but I'll never call her the lily maid again.

As she held on to the dock, her heart was singing. I kept my head, she was exulting, I kept my head and brought the boat safely across the lake in one of Champlain's wild windstorms.

There was a rush of feet on the steep graveled roadway. Bates and Ray came pounding down to the dock.

"What the deuce were you girls thinking of to cross the lake in a blow like this?" Ray demanded.

"Aunt Charlotte had a bad fall," Kit explained briefly. "We came for Dr. Gardner. She's badly hurt."

"My gosh!" Ray exclaimed, in startled sympathy.

"Oh, Bates, I was so frightened," Elaine was sobbing again. "I thought we were going to drown. You can't imagine how awful it was."

Bates put his arm around Elaine's trembling shoulders. "It's all right now," he comforted her as if she were a little child. "You're safe. Don't think of it any more." He looked down at Kit, who was still in the boat. "Bravo, Kit," he said. "You did a wonderful job!" Then he turned to Ray who was helping Kit make the boat fast.

"I'll take Elaine up to the Edwards'," he said. "Then I'll get Dr. Gardner. You bring Kit when you've tied up the boat."

Kit handed the mooring lines up to Ray. He bent down and patted her on the head. "Gee, Brick Top," he said, "you're a wonder. We were watching through Cliff Edwards' binoculars. Of course we couldn't tell who was in the boat. Sometimes the darn thing disappeared entirely behind a whale of a wave, and we held our breath until it came up again. We'd have passed out if we'd known who was in it. I'll say you're a super sailor, Brick Top."

Kit sat on the dock, limp and worn out, and let her legs dangle down into the *Kittyken*. She felt the glow of her triumph over wind and waves, but she confessed to herself that she felt a little wobbly. And she couldn't ignore the question that kept beating in the back of her mind. Had Bates taken care of Elaine and left Kit to Ray only because Elaine was in greater need, and Ray knew more about boats than he did, or was Elaine beginning to be of special interest to him?

"Come on, Brick Top," Ray urged briskly. "You can't sit around in this north wind in those wet clothes. Come on up to the Edwards' and you can borrow some of Sally's duds while yours dry out."

Kit didn't believe she could walk up Westport hill, but Ray pulled her to her feet and took her arm.

"Dr. Gardner will probably drive down and over the bridge," he said, "but we can't get back across the lake until the wind dies down, possibly around sundown."

17

A Very Special Passenger

On his return in the late afternoon, Dr. Gardner telephoned the Edwards'. Aunt Charlotte was comfortable, he reported, though she was suffering from a slight concussion. He had given her an anti-tetanus injection, taken a couple of stitches in the cut on the side of her head, and ordered her to bed until he returned at the end of the week. Kit need not worry, he told her; her great-aunt would be all right, thanks to her niece's prompt and courageous action in summoning him without delay. He agreed that it was unnecessary to interrupt Mr. and Mrs. Turner's vacation.

As Ray had predicted, the wind died down at sunset. Bates suggested a shift in passengers. He would ride home with Kit, and Elaine with Ray. Though the wind was calm now, great swells were still rolling in from the north. Kit sat in the bobbing *Kittyken* and watched Elaine and Ray push off. Bates threw in the lines and dropped nimbly down beside her, in spite of his lame leg. Kit, in a sweater and skirt of Sally's, touched the starter. One day of her father's Canadian vacation would have been spoiled by worry, she was sure, if he had known of this trip. Here she was, as she had dreamed of being, running the *Kittyken* with Bates as a passenger.

As they approached the entrance to the harbor, she and Bates shared the startling beauty of the gorgeous sunset. As she had expected, the wind from the north had blown away the last vestige of the sticky haze. Beyond Westport, the black mass of the mountains stood out sharp and clear. All about them, the heaving surface of the lake, stained with the brilliant colors of the sunset, repeated the glory of the sky.

"I don't believe there are very many places in the whole world where sunsets are more beautiful," Kit remarked.

Bates nodded, not turning from the glorious spectacle behind them. "You love it, don't you, Kit?"

"I've spent every summer of my life here. Do you blame me?"

They were out in the broad lake now. Kit shivered a little, feeling the sharp cold through Sally's sweater. "It feels as if the mercury had dropped about twenty degrees."

"This is where I'd offer you my jacket, if I were so fortunate as to be wearing one," Bates said.

Moving nearer to her on the broad seat, he put his arm around her and drew her to him. The wool of his shirt was soft and warm against Kit's cheek. With an effort, she forced herself to breathe slowly and evenly, hoping he would not feel the staccato racing of her heart. Its rapid beat throbbed so loudly that she was sure he must hear it. She wanted to say something, anything to distract his attention, but her stupid mind seemed suddenly empty.

What would Bates think of her? He had taken the weeping Elaine up to the Edwards', leaving Kit to Ray. Now he was with Kit, but she could not know how much either circumstance was the result of his own choice. Since the boys had come in Ray's boat, it was natural that Bates should be the one to accompany Kit.

The flaming brilliance of the sunset was fading now. The *Kittyken,* cutting cleaning through the great rollers, ploughed steadily along the diagonal course Kit had set.

Bates tightened his arm, giving Kit a quick little hug. "Feeling warmer?" he asked, smiling down at her.

"Oh, yes, thanks," Kit answered quickly. Searching desperately for something to say, she added, "This is the first time I've had the *Kittyken* out alone. My father thinks it's not safe for me to take her out by myself."

Bates threw back his head and laughed. "I wish he'd seen you crossing over this afternoon," he said. "He'd never worry about you again."

"I hope he'll feel that way when he hears about it."

Kit had had the boat's running lights on for some time. Twilight was already hugging the eastern shore, though it was still fairly light on the water. In the west a pale lemon glow deepened above the jagged outline of the Palisades. They looked like cardboard cutout hills, Kit thought, sharply outlined in the clear atmosphere, and propped up there, black, against the luminous saffron sky.

"There goes Ray into the Lesters'," she said, and pointed. Ray's stern light described a wide arc, and then the red and green of his port and starboard lights glowed, as he came up alongside the Lesters' dock. A few minutes later, she swung the *Kittyken* round to come up neatly to her own dock.

They could see a bobbing light descending through the

dusk, and when they came alongside, Ken was standing there waving a lantern.

"Home is the sailor," he shouted, "and about time! When I got home, and Martha told me what Kit had done, I was flabbergasted. Fortunately, Dr. Gardner came along shortly after and told us she was safe at the Edwards'."

He put down his lantern and reached for the lines as Bates handed them up to him. He made the boat fast and jumped in to hand out the oars and other paraphernalia. Bates pulled himself up on the dock and reached down to give Kit a hand.

"Kit is to be congratulated," he said, his deep voice making his words sound even more formal, "on her remarkable performance in bringing the *Kittyken* safely through such a windstorm."

"My hat's off to you, Kit," Ken said heartily.

They had just finished stowing away the gear when they heard Ray cutting across from the Lesters'. They waited until he pulled in to the dock.

"I thought I'd run you home, Bates, if you like," he offered.

"Come on up to the house," Ken invited. "Martha has hot coffee waiting."

Ray cut his engine and made his boat fast to the dock. They followed Ken and his lantern up to the house. It was cold in the thick darkness under the trees. The air was sharp with balsam and rich with the smell of damp earth. The stone steps were cold and slippery with dew. Kit was shivering and so tired she could hardly stumble up the path. Ray took her arm and half pulled her up the steps. Bates followed along in the rear.

Martha came running to the door to hug Kit tight against her warm softness. "Kit, Kit," she said, "I'm glad to have you back safe, child."

"You should have seen Kit come across the lake in the teeth of that gale," Ray told them enthusiastically. "The girl's a real sailor—and that's for sure."

"How is Aunt Charlotte?" Kit asked Martha.

"She's asleep," Martha answered. "Dr. Gardner gave her a sedative. I'm going to sleep in her room tonight just to keep an eye on her, but Dr. Gardner said she'll be all right in a few days."

They gathered around the fire to drink Martha's steaming hot coffee and eat big pieces of her fluffy golden sponge cake. But even as the hot liquid warmed her, Kit felt her eyes closing. She hardly knew how she said good night to Bates and Ray and stumbled up to bed.

"That Only I Remember"

Kit spent the following days helping Martha nurse Aunt Charlotte. At first, under the sedative the doctor had left for her, she drowsed through the days half conscious. The third morning when sedation was discontinued, she was completely clear in her mind and demanding to know what had happened. Martha told her about her fall and Kit's adventure in summoning the doctor.

Aunt Charlotte was almost embarrassingly grateful. "It's been hard for me to understand modern girls in their shorts and jeans," she told Kit, "but I can be thankful for their courage and self-reliance, if you're a sample."

After lunch Ken went off to Bud Summers' to help exercise the Morgan horse his grandmother had given him for his birthday. Kit was tempted to go too. She had heard about Morgan horses all her life and had seen them at Middlebury on the Morgan Horse Farm where the big statue of Justin Morgan, the horse who had founded the strain, was a prominent feature of the front lawn, and she was eager to have a look at Bud's birthday gift. But she felt that in her mother's absence she should stay with Aunt Charlotte, so, with a sigh, she had let Ken go off without her, more than ever convinced that boys had all the best of it, for of course no one would expect Ken to nurse Aunt Charlotte or to relieve Martha of any of her duties.

She went up to be with the patient while Martha went on with her housework. Sitting with Aunt Charlotte while Martha was busy, Kit had been surprised at the swift growth of their mutual respect and understanding. Often Aunt Charlotte talked about her girlhood in Virginia, about her marriage and the loss of her husband in the First World War, and the death of her only son in a riding accident. Aunt Charlotte had borne her sorrow well. It was contrary to her code of conduct to permit her tragedy to sadden others. Once Kit had been tempted to tell her how she felt about Bates.

After a time Aunt Charlotte complained of a pain in her head and Kit gave her a couple of aspirin tablets. When at last she fell asleep, Kit tiptoed out of the room, almost giddy with the feeling of release from the quiet and inactivity of the sickroom.

At the bottom of the stairs His Nibs greeted her with little whines and whimpers of pleasure, his stub of a tail whipping furiously around in circles. He ran toward the door, then back to Kit, looking up at her with bright brown eyes that asked as clearly as words to be taken for a romp.

With His Nibs capering about her feet, Kit went into the kitchen. "Aunt Charlotte is asleep," she told Martha. "I'm going to take His Nibs for a little run. I won't be long."

"You go right ahead," Martha drawled. "I'll keep an eye on Mrs. Penfield. I'm nearly through here anyway."

Kit, with His Nibs cavorting in front of her, went out the back door. His Nibs bounded ahead, chasing back and forth from one side of the road to the other, in frenzied pursuit of one tantalizing scent after another.

The last couple of days hadn't been much fun for him, cooped up in the house, so Kit let him run free, whistling him back only when he strayed too widely afield or lagged too far behind. There was no one to be seen when they passed the open gates of Thendara. Bates was probably putting the finishing touches on his script, which he planned to have ready to show her father on his return.

The next weeks would be busy ones for the whole group. There would be costumes to borrow or make, tickets to sell, props to assemble, lines to memorize, rehearsals—all climaxing in the performances the last week in August and on Labor Day.

Just around the bend where the road dipped in a long gentle slope toward the Summers' place, Kit saw a horse and rider approaching at a gallop. As they drew nearer, Kit realized that the rider was Ray and, at the same moment, His Nibs dashed at the horse, barking furiously in a series of high piercing yelps. Kit stood still, her heart beating wildly in terror, as the horse reared and bolted past her down the rutted road. His Nibs came back, his triumphant swagger proclaiming unmistakably that, as her protector, he had successfully routed an enemy. When she began to scold him, he looked at her in such injured bewilderment that she almost laughed.

Evidently Ray had kept control of the Morgan, guiding her safely around the curves, for Kit could see him now up near the farm where the road switched back parallel to the lake road. In a few minutes he had made the full circle and was coming toward her again at a walk.

"Hold that ferocious beast of yours," he called out. "He nearly gave me a heart attack."

But Kit could see that Ray was really very proud of the way he had handled the horse. She had snapped the leash on His Nibs and now she drew him close to her side.

The little Morgan was truly a beautiful animal. Her smooth chestnut coat glistened in the sun. She tossed her small finely shaped head and danced a little as she came toward Kit and His Nibs.

"She's beautiful," Kit said. "What's her name?"

"Ellen," Ray answered, "and she's a sweetheart. Gentle as a kitten, except when she's frightened by a wild animal like that dog of yours."

"He certainly gave me a fright," Kit answered. "I didn't know you were such a fine horseman, Ray, and I was terrified."

Pleased, Ray reined in alongside Kit and dismounted. Kit tied His Nibs to a fence post and moved slowly toward the mare. She held out her hand and Ellen nuzzled it with soft lips that tickled a little. "I wish I had a lump of sugar," Kit lamented.

"Want to ride her back to the Summers'?" Ray offered. "I'll take His Nibs."

Kit needed no urging. Ray gave her a hand as she mounted, and in a moment she was trotting down the road toward her own house. She knew she should turn around and head for the Summers', but the little Morgan's easy gait was too strong a temptation. "I'll just ride around by the farm," Kit thought. Tightening the reins, she touched the mare with her knee. Ellen broke into an easy canter. Kit felt as gay and carefree as His Nibs. Just as she came up to Thendara, the Jaguar came down the driveway and stopped at the gates to let her pass. Bates was driving, and Elaine sat beside him.

"Kit," Elaine shrieked, "where did you get that beautiful horse?"

Kit rode up to the car. "She belongs to Bud Summers," she explained. "A birthday present from his grandmother. I'm riding her back home."

"She's a . . ." Bates began.

"The script is finished," Elaine interrupted importantly. "Bates let me print The End in red crayon. We're calling a rehearsal tomorrow, and I'm taking him home to the dinner he didn't get the other day."

Kit remembered that before Aunt Charlotte's fall, Elaine had come over to borrow some eggs for a cake she intended to bake because Bates was to be a dinner guest at the Lesters'.

"Elaine's been helping to type parts," Bates explained. "We're calling the first meeting tomorrow morning at ten o'clock—at my house. Parts to be assigned, readings from script. Pass the word along, will you, and we'll tell anyone we meet."

Kit nodded. "Ten o'clock." She waved and rode off. The Jaguar turned toward the Lesters'.

Kit yearned to follow it. She had felt that the play was a project belonging to her and Bates, and now Elaine had stepped in, and it was, *"We're* calling a rehearsal." She could imagine Elaine, blond curls gleaming in the candlelight, displaying her charm as a hostess, her skill as a cook, as she cut her delicious-looking cake. All week Kit had hugged to herself the feeling of Bates's arm around her shoulders, dreaming of him as she sat with Aunt Charlotte. When Bates was with her, the world was a different place—warm, alive, full of color. All her senses seemed keener—the perfume of flowers stronger, music sweeter, colors brighter. When Bates was not there, reality faded into a vague emptiness, as if the world stood still and all things were under a spell, awaiting his return, like the Sleeping Beauty, to wake to life again.

She rode slowly back to the Summers'. She had never known such jealousy before. Now it surged over her, hot and consuming. But she couldn't help it. She had never found Elaine congenial though she had tried to be fair to her, especially since Elaine had so pluckily accompanied her on the wild trip across the lake. But now she almost hated her—blue eyes, blond curls, and all.

Unbidden, a picture from the *Oz* books of her childhood flashed into her mind. It was an illustration of the doughty little wizard slashing one of the vegetable people down through the middle, while juice and seeds splashed out, as when one cuts through a cucumber. She could see herself slashing through Elaine with a long scimitar in the same fashion, and she was amazed and dismayed at the thrill of savage joy the picture gave her.

At the Summers' she dismounted. Bud was delighted with her enthusiasm over the little Morgan. He was like a child with a new bicycle, Kit thought—pleased with his playmates' admiration for his new toy, but hardly able to try it himself because of lending it to the eager, envious circle.

"We have to be heading for home," she told Ray, stretching out her hand for His Nibs's leash.

Ray held it out of her reach. "I'll walk you home."

They said good-by to Bud and followed the prancing little dog along the rutted road up the hill and around the curve and down past Thendara.

"I understand the Cunninghams are giving a big shindig at the club the night after the play," Ray said.

Kit nodded, and suddenly suspecting that he was going to ask to be her date, began to babble, "It's going to be quite an affair—an orchestra from Boston and . . ."

Undaunted, Ray broke in. "How about it, Kit? Be my girl?"

But Kit gave a shriek and began to run down the driveway, for standing at the back door was her father's car. Now she would have to explain about taking the *Kittyken* across the lake and face her father's possible anger.

19

Mrs. Howard Says No

The next few days had for Kit the dizzying effect of a roller coaster, dashing her from joyous heights to depths of gloom. Her mother's permission to keep His Nibs and her pride over the responsible way in which Kit had nursed Aunt Charlotte more than made up for the good times Kit had given up. Her father heard the boys' tale of her masterly handling of the *Kittyken* with open astonishment, but he was proud of her too. Kit was elated when, instead of scolding, he conceded that she had earned the right to take the boat out by herself.

She was delighted with her present of several pairs of English knee-high socks to wear with her Bermudas. Mr. and Mrs. Turner had thoroughly enjoyed what they laughingly called their second honeymoon. They appeared rested and refreshed and were eager to join in the plans of the young people. Her mother agreed that Mrs. Phoebe was to be permitted to raise her family unmolested in her latest precarious perch. And even without being asked, Mrs. Turner offered her services as wardrobe mistress for the pageant.

Mr. Turner promised to devote as much time as necessary

during the next week to the promotion of the benefit. He read Bates's script, and there was a hint of flattering astonishment in his hearty congratulations on an unusually fine job. Now that he was assured that, if the actors were any good at all, the performance promised to be exceedingly worthwhile, he could promote it with unrestrained enthusiasm.

In the midst of a discussion about the printing of the posters and tickets, he turned to Kit. "By the way, has anyone consulted Molly Howard about all this?" he asked.

They admitted somewhat sheepishly that no one had.

"Well, what are you waiting for?" he asked impatiently. "Surely you can see that it's impossible to proceed any further without Mrs. Howard's permission? And we ought to place this printing order without delay. Kit, suppose you go see Molly Howard this afternoon?"

Kit heard him with dismay. She was shy with strangers, and the thought of explaining her project to the woman it was designed to help almost paralyzed her. She remembered now Martha's half-heard warning about Molly Howard's pride and independence. If she found the idea of a benefit performance under the auspices of comparative strangers offensive, and with a dignified but final, "No, thank you," refused to permit it, Kit was sure she would be completely inadequate in the role of tactful persuader.

Before she could voice her feelings, Bates spoke. "Let me drive you over, Kit," he suggested, and added, with an understanding smile, "and perhaps lend a little moral support, in case it's needed."

"Oh, Bates, would you?" Kit's face showed her relief. "I'll be everlastingly grateful."

With a nod, Bates indicated the papers on which Mr. Turner had written the copy for the tickets and posters. "What would you think, sir, of our leaving these with the printer on the way back, if the lady agrees?"

"Good idea. In the meantime, I'll plan some stories for the local press and get in touch with Dan Hughes of the Burlington radio station and a couple of other men in Rutland and over on the New York side to see what we can do about some time on the air."

"I'll stop for you right after lunch," Bates told Kit as he limped out to his car.

He was in a gay mood when he returned some time later. He had been tremendously set up by Mr. Turner's sincere and enthusiastic reaction to the script, and the exhilaration remained. Even without a word from her mother, Kit for once had decided against shorts, and she wore a blue linen dress that showed her graceful figure to advantage. In spite of her trepidation over the approaching interview with Mrs. Howard, she felt a singing happiness as she settled herself on the red leather seat beside Bates.

He wore no hat, and the wind had tousled his black hair a little just as it had that first morning on the river, but the bony planes and sharp angles of his thin face were tanned now, and the long, thin fingers on the wheel were brown. Sitting beside him—he was head and shoulders above her —Kit felt unusually small and feminine. He smiled at her in an especially intimate way as they made the turn around the big pine tree. Kit thought there was less pain and a lot more zest for living in his shadowed blue eyes.

" 'She was a phantom of delight,' " he quoted. "You look

luscious enough to eat, Kit. Blue suits you, my sweet Kate."

He was only echoing her father's oft-repeated name for her, Kit knew, but it sounded so different in Bates's deep voice, with Bates smiling at her in that you-and-I-all-alone-in-the-world fashion. She had a heady sensation of lightness, as if she were floating dreamily in space.

"Best thing I ever did was lose that oar," Bates went on. "Getting to know you and all the crowd has made a big difference not only in my summer, but I'm beginning to think in my whole life as well. I've really forgotten now that I'm any different from what I was before my illness, and I've enjoyed myself without reservation, as I used to. My poor long-suffering parents are so delighted they'd like to buy the Gunnerson place."

Buy Thendara! With a jolt, Kit realized that she no longer missed Marge—indeed she hadn't thought of her for days. Oh, dear, was she a disloyal friend—or was out of sight, out of mind the usual way with most people?

"I've had such a good time researching and writing our pageant that I've definitely decided to take the workshop course at Yale, and I'm looking forward to it now as something I really want to do, not just something to fill up the time of a man who can't go out for football or track."

"Oh, Bates, I'm so glad." If Bates had not been so intent on his driving and on describing his own feelings, he would have seen the adoration in Kit's face as she gazed up at him. But his eyes were on the road as he went on: "Even though I vowed not to follow in my father's footsteps, I may do something with some kind of historical writing, after all. And in the hackneyed words of the sob sisters, I owe it all to

—a lost oar and the girl who returned it. I'm grateful for so much more than an oar. I'll never forget you, my sweet Kate."

Though his eyes were smiling and he spoke lightly, Kit knew Bates meant what he said. But with a sudden pang so sharp that she almost cried out, came the stabbing thought that he was talking to her as he might talk to any good friend, and certainly with no special romantic interest.

Almost immediately this suspicion was confirmed when Bates boasted, "And I who thought girls would never again bother with me, have a date for the party after the show with the star, the most popular girl on the lake shore. And Elaine has promised to come up to Yale too, later this fall. So I'm not doing badly—am I, my sweet Kate?"

The pain seemed to swell and spread until it was a dull numbing ache. Somehow Kit managed stiff, lifeless replies to Bates's questions. She knew that pain was waiting to seize her again, but she clung to the numb feeling as one does to the effect of novocaine during dentistry. Somehow she must get through the interview with Molly Howard and home again without letting Bates suspect how he had hurt her.

In Bristol, as they were driving past the quiet village green, shaded by tall old elms and with its round bandstand gleaming white against the green, Bates exclaimed, "Look, there's Guy Howard."

On a homemade contraption of boards and wheels, Guy was zooming towards them down the street. Bates stopped the car and called to him.

"Hi there, big boy," Bates greeted him, as Guy braked with his foot to stop with a flourish alongside the car.

"Hi," Guy returned a trifle shyly, and then with a mischievous gleam in his hazel eyes, he asked, "How's your girl this afternoon, mister? Her heart strong enough to watch us dive?"

The "how's your girl?" pricked through Kit's numbness, but she managed a smile. "Hello, Guy," she said, "my heart's not doing at all well today, and anyway we came to see your mother. Will you tell us how to find your house?"

"Tain't our house, it's my aunt's," Guy explained, curiosity plain on his expressive face. He indicated directions with a wave of a small brown hand and prepared to follow them as swiftly as his homemade scooter would allow.

Guy's aunt, Mrs. Clark, was a younger edition of Molly Howard. She invited Bates and Kit into a small immaculate living room, furnished with a sofa and winged chair, covered with clean, much-laundered slip covers, and a chest, a drop-leaf table, and some old chairs that even Kit knew would make an antique dealer's mouth water.

When they were comfortably seated, she went away to call her sister.

If Molly Howard was puzzled by this unexpected call, she masked it well with quiet courtesy. Though Kit had been rehearsing what she intended to say, she found it difficult to begin. Finally she blurted out, "Please forgive us, Mrs. Howard, if we seem to be meddling in your affairs, but ever since we met Guy and his brothers—you must be proud of such handsome, well-brought-up boys—we have wanted to do something to help. Bates has written a—a pageant, I suppose you'd call it—which we would like to give at Thendara as a benefit performance for you and the boys."

Molly Howard's first reaction was one of complete astonishment. In the moment of silence during which she was trying to recover her breath, Kit could hear Guy's voice raised in protest at being shut out of the living room when, after all, the callers were special friends of his. His aunt was doing her best to quiet him.

"It is very, very kind of you to take such an interest in me and the boys," Molly Howard said slowly. "It seems to me most unusual for young people to be so concerned about the troubles of others, especially comparative strangers."

Her blue eyes were shiny with tears as she went on, bending toward them in her earnestness. "How can I make you understand what your wanting to do this for us means to me? It gives me courage I need so desperately, and the thought of it will bolster up my spirit whenever I need it in the days to come, for I shall never forget it."

Her voice was trembling with emotion. To give her time to pull herself together, Bates switched the emphasis to the practical side. "Then we may go ahead with our preparations, Mrs. Howard?" he asked.

Slowly she shook her head. "Please believe that I shall always be grateful," she said. "You have helped me more than you could possibly know. Somehow the boys and I will manage." She stretched out her hands toward them in a gesture Kit felt was unusual for this self-contained woman. "Please, please understand," she begged. My boys must grow up in this community, and for their sake I cannot accept the public charity of such a benefit."

Kit tried her best to persuade Mrs. Howard to change her mind, and Bates seconded her ably, but Molly, though touched and grateful, was firm.

Kit and Bates drove halfway home in dejected silence.

"Well," Bates said bitterly at last, "there goes our pageant. I might have known it would be like this. Just my rotten luck."

"Nonsense," Kit snapped back, on the verge of tears herself, "it's no more your bad luck than mine." Her voice shook a little, as she remembered how she had hoped to help Molly Howard buy a home for Guy, Monkey, and the others, and to wear the once-hated aqua dress as Bates Cunningham's special date. The summer which, in spite of her expectations to the contrary, had begun in such a happy glow of romance was ending in misery and failure.

"That only I remember—" she quoted sadly to herself and finished the line grimly, "—that only you admire." What Bates admired was Elaine's golden curls.

20

Ray to the Rescue

Surprisingly enough, it was Ray who persuaded Molly Howard to agree to the benefit. He came along in his boat in
the early evening when Kit was sitting alone on the flat
rocks. She had escaped from the house as soon as possible
after dinner. Her attempts to hide her unhappiness had
been heavy going, and she thought she couldn't bear it if
anyone noticed and commented on her low spirits. She
wanted to get away by herself and nurse her misery in soli-
tude.

In her present state of mind there was a poignant sadness
in the beauty of the summer evening. The sun had set, but
the afterglow lingered pale saffron above the dark mass of
the mountains. Their shadow edged the opaque ice-white
of the lake with a band of black along the opposite shore.
The blinker on Diamond Island winked through the dusk,
and one by one lights began to glow like fireflies on the long
dark finger of Thompson's Point.

The smell of burning wood from the fire on the hearth
back at the house was sharp on the west wind. Though the
rocks were still warm from the sun, a chill rose from the wa-

ter. Kit shivered and drew her sweater around her. For the moment only the trills of birds, calling and answering in sleepy good night, broke the twilight hush.

Bird-song! Kit put her head down on the rocky ledge of the retaining wall and let the tears come. She had been sobbing for some time when she became aware that the sputter of the outboard motor she had subconsciously been hearing had increased in volume and then stopped. She lifted her face, wet with tears, as Ray Tabor stepped from his boat and came up beside her.

"Brick Top!" Ray exclaimed in embarrassed distress. "What—what's the trouble?"

He looked so unhappy that Kit almost laughed. He's wishing he were a thousand miles from here, she thought.

"Anything I can do?" Ray asked uncertainly.

"There's nothing anyone can do," Kit said slowly. She couldn't tell Ray that she was weeping because the night was so beautiful and she had lost her first love. She thought quickly—Molly Howard and the pageant! When she explained, Ray's uneasiness dropped from him and he was immediately eager to try to set things right.

"Don't cry another tear, Brick Top," he said, standing above her and patting her tenderly on the head. "Everything's going to be all right. We'll manage to get around Mrs. Howard somehow."

He sat down beside her on the rocks and, as she was still sniffing a little, he offered her his handkerchief. Kit took it and blew her nose. She had been crying hard and she knew her nose was red and her eyes swollen. How romantic can you get, she thought with a giggle.

"That's the girl, Brick Top," Ray said, relieved. "By

George," he slapped his knee, "I've just had a brilliant idea! We'll call the pageant a memorial to William Howard, a brave man. Molly can hardly turn that down."

Ray proved to be right. On this basis, Mrs. Howard was proud to accept the William Howard Memorial program.

The whole crowd immediately went to work. Their days and a considerable part of their nights were completely devoted to pageant business. Kit felt guilty if she even stole a moment to go aquaplaning in back of Ray's boat. Bud complained that the Morgan was growing restive for lack of exercise.

Summer people along the lake shore, residents of the City of Vergennes, outlying farms and surrounding towns, all were extremely generous. The list of patrons, each of whom had contributed donations of ten dollars or more—and most of the gifts were more—filled several pages of the program. Kit was elated at the size of the checks she received from her mother and Aunt Charlotte.

People were generous, too, about lending much-prized old uniforms, dresses, bonnets, and cherished antiques.

Kit went to the Turner home first. Like so many Vermonters, Dick Turner had gone off as a young man to seek a career elsewhere. The only member of the family still in Vergennes was an elderly cousin who lived down beyond the schoolhouse. She not only offered to lend several linsey-woolsey dresses of the colonial era, a chest and a drop-leaf table, gleaming with the patina of years of loving care, but she gave them hints as to others who might be willing to part with cherished heirlooms for the duration of the pageant.

In the house on Main Street that General Strong, who had led the American forces so valiantly in the Battle of Plattsburg in 1814, had built back in 1796, his great-great-great-granddaughter invited them into the dining room to see the French wall paper that had been on the walls all the one hundred and sixty-odd years since the house had been built. The young people were interested in her stories of the many heirlooms among which she lived. She was a generous patron and delighted them by lending them a pair of English boarding swords which had been used during the Battle of Plattsburg and presented to General Strong by Commodore Thomas Macdonough, who had received them from a British captain after the surrender of the English.

Another loan which appealed to the boys was that of an old musket which bore the mark of the bullet which at the Battle of Bunker Hill had wounded the several times great-grandfather of one of their friends in Vergennes.

In Vergennes and the surrounding country, calling on people who proudly recounted family reminiscences connected with two hundred years of their country's history and who lived surrounded by cherished mementoes of proud events of the past, Kit began for the first time to be really interested in her own ancestors.

The careful thrift that had preserved these objects so lovingly to be handed down from generation to generation, reminded her of her father's joking remark about the New England tradition of "Eat it up, wear it out, make it do, do without."

In giving her leads about antiques that might be used in the pageant, people ran down family connections in the same fashion that Aunt Charlotte and her mother's relatives talked about "kissin' kin" when Kit visited them in Virginia. "Sarah Adams—" someone would say, "she was an

Allen, you know, and her mother's father was one of the Ferrisburg Beaches." Apartment-dwelling Kit, who had grown up in a fairly rootless, ever-changing metropolitan circle, began to appreciate another way of life. She began to understand, as she never had before, the continuity in the lives of these people whose forebears had woven into the fabric of her country its proud traditions of human dignity, self-reliance, and freedom. And she came to the realization that the debt she owed to them could only be discharged by holding fast to what they had achieved and by passing it along to future generations.

Bates worked all day and far into the night rehearsing, directing, coordinating the whole performance. He seemed to thrive on it. Kit had never seen him so happy.

The narration was no problem. His deep, resonant voice filled the Gunnerson living room as he read the script which linked the scenes and tableaux in a running history of the Champlain country.

The first scene showed Ray, handsome in helmet and breastplate borrowed from the museum at Ticonderoga, as Samuel Champlain, surrounded by his Algonquins and Hurons in war paint and feathers. Until she saw Ray striding about the stage, Kit had hardly realized that in the early days of our country, the sun had shone on armor as well as on painted savages. Ray had finally been persuaded to say a few lines as the first white man to view the beauty of Lake Champlain.

Then, in his deep dramatic voice, Bates told the story of the early settlements, the building of the forts at Crown Point and Ticonderoga, and the burning of Arnold's fleet.

Elaine, beautiful in colonial costume, coquetted with

Benedict Arnold, congratulating him on his cleverness in outwitting the British. Later, in one of Cousin Hattie's linsey-woolsey gowns, she was a New Hampshire pioneer woman standing bravely shoulder to shoulder with her husband, as the Yorkers tried to dispossess them of their land, and Ethan Allen and his Green Mountain boys came to the rescue in the nick of time. In another scene, as a demure Vermont maiden, she encouraged Ken, as Commodore Macdonough, while he built his boats by the falls of the Otter. And later, she fêted him and General Strong after the Battle of Plattsburg.

Kit was so busy that she had no time for sadness or jealousy or dreams of romance. Like Ray, she had refused to have anything to do with parts that required any great acting ability or involved the memorization of many lines. She did appear in a couple of the tableaux in which she was not required to speak; she helped her mother with the costumes and the quick changes Elaine and others had to make; and she assisted Bud, who was in charge of props. She helped with make-up, painted scenery, and even lent a hand with the lighting effects of which Ken was so proud.

Because of Bates and the Howards, the success of the performance meant much to her. She would ask no more of the summer, she told herself sternly, than that the pageant be a smash hit.

21

Gifts of Summer

"Put that down at once, you naughty dog," said Kit crossly, as she rescued her bedroom slipper from His Nibs, who was rushing madly around her room in an excess of puppy spirits, grabbing anything he could find to toss and shake and chew.

Kit was tired. It was the late afternoon of the day after the last performance of the pageant. She was lying on her bed, feeling a letdown now that the excitement was over and their goal achieved. She would have to get up in a moment and begin to dress for Bates's party.

To cheers and whistles and prolonged applause, the heavy red portières dividing the Gunnerson living room from the dining room had swept closed on the last performance of the pageant. Each night an enthusiastic audience had cheered Bates as author and Elaine as star.

Molly Howard, surrounded by her handsome sons, had looked very pretty in a dress that matched the color of her eyes. The president of the bank in Vergennes, who had volunteered to take charge of the funds and to arrange for the purchase of the little house, had telephoned that morning to announce the gratifying news that they had more than met the down payment.

Molly Howard would be able to keep her family together. She had accepted a position in Fisher's Department Store, and the older boys were assured of after-school jobs. Guy and Monkey would return to school and the companions they had so sorely missed.

The Howards were deeply grateful. The radiance of their quiet happiness at the prospect of being together again in a home of their own at last more than paid the young people for all their hard work.

Kit had not stopped Ray the next time he had made an opportunity to ask her to be his date for the party. She was going to wear the aqua dress, if not with the joyousness with which she had hoped to wear it as Bates's partner, still not with the dread she had anticipated at the beginning of the summer.

It had been quite a summer. She knew she would always remember it. It had given her one tangible present in the shape of His Nibs, and many other worthwhile benefits that were intangible. She wondered if there was always a time—a summer, perhaps—in every girl's life to which she could look back as a sort of dividing line between childhood and womanhood. It had been that way with her certainly. She had been a little girl at the beginning of the summer—a retarded one perhaps, according to Aunt Charlotte.

She had met Bates and known the thrilling excitement and sweetness of first love. Although her feeling had not been reciprocated, she knew she would always remember Bates. He would return to her in a line of poetry, in the beauty of a sunset, in the tilt of a tousled black head.

Her parents had become not just Mother and Dad, concerned only with her well-being, but individuals with their own hopes and failures. She had come to know and love Aunt Charlotte.

She was still a little bitter about Elaine, who had taken Bates from her, but she was honest enough to admit that even from Elaine she had learned that one can get along with people of different tastes and temperament.

"It takes all kinds of people to make the world go round," she said aloud, as she got off the bed and began to dress. "Some like onions and some don't." She would probably never find Elaine congenial, but she would never forget the stubborn courage the timid, posing, baby-talking girl had displayed in accompanying her across the lake.

Perhaps best of all, she had learned not to be afraid to be herself. She no longer faced a social affair with a sinking heart. If she was doomed to be a wallflower tonight—or next winter at school dances—she could face even that with equanimity. But, paradoxically, having achieved this enviable indifference, she knew instinctively that she would not lack for partners.

She took the aqua dress from its hanger and slipped it over her head. Its long, slim lines, flaring into fullness below the hips, accented her lovely figure. As she bent nearer the mirror, a faint stir of excitement began to tingle within her. Her eyes were deep blue, her hair was a flaming glory above her white skin and the deep blue-green of her dress.

She rummaged in the drawer of her dressing table to find some long-discarded pancake make-up and very carefully smoothed it over the freckles on her nose. Then with an eyebrow pencil she had secretly bought for this occasion, she very deliberately darkened her brows. She could not fail to see that the girl who looked back at her from the mirror was attractive. She felt a warm wave of excitement and anticipation.

For a long time she stood there gazing into the mirror. Who am I? What am I? she thought in dizzy confusion. I am one person to Mother, and another to Dad. I am one girl to Bates, and an entirely different one to Ray. Which is the real me? How can I tell, when even to myself I am one girl today and another tomorrow?

There was a knock on the door and Aunt Charlotte came into the room.

"My dear," Aunt Charlotte said, as Kit came toward her, "how lovely you look!" There was a trace of astonishment mingled with the real affection in Aunt Charlotte's voice.

She held out her hands filled with glittering ice-blue stones. "These aquamarines belonged to your great-grandmother, Kit," she said, using the nickname for the first time. "I want you to have them. I thought you might like to wear them tonight."

There were two wide bracelets, a necklace, and earrings. Kit put them on, surprised at her own feminine delight in them.

"They are most becoming," Aunt Charlotte said, gratified by Kit's evident pleasure. "I have never seen you look so charming."

"Thank you," Kit said, and kissed her lightly.

Aunt Charlotte gave her great-niece a quick hug. "Either you have changed a great deal this summer, or I have at last come to a better understanding of the modern generation."

"A little of both, I think, Aunt Charlotte," Kit said, laughing.

Ken whistled in startled amazement when Kit came downstairs. Mr. Turner jumped up from his chair. "My sweet Kate!" he exclaimed. "Tonight you are extra beautiful!"

He beamed on her so proudly that Kit was touched. There was a momentary flash of tears in her eyes as she turned to her mother. Mrs. Turner drew her aside a moment.

"You've made us all very happy this summer, Kit," she said seriously. "Your father and I are so proud that you are growing up to be the lovely, thoughtful woman we want you to be."

She kissed Kit and then added, with a gleam of mischief in her eyes, "Now if you just behave as well as you look . . ."

"Mother!" Kit protested, laughing.

She was still laughing as Ray came in.

"Brick Top!" he exclaimed, oblivious of the admiring circle around Kit. "You're a knockout! Am I ever a lucky guy!"

He looked very handsome himself, his white tuxedo jacket setting off his tanned skin, dark hair and eyes. His good looks were sturdy and down to earth, not romantic in the Lord Byron fashion of Bates Cunningham. Kit sighed a last lingering sigh and then she smiled at Ray and followed him out to his car.

"You sure bowled me over tonight, Brick Top," Ray said later as they drew up to the club house. "I'm going to be mighty proud when you come up to Dartmouth as my girl for the winter carnival."

"Thanks, Ray," Kit said lightly. She knew she could never feel about Ray as she had about Bates, but there was no reason why she should not enjoy his friendship and that of other boys. "Thanks, Ray," she repeated, turning her glowing face to his. "It will be fun to be your girl for the carnival. I'll look forward to it, but I warn you I won't be anyone's girl exclusively for a long, long time."

She knew somehow that tonight she would be sought after, cut in on, what Aunt Charlotte would call the belle of the ball. She drew a quick breath at these dizzying thoughts. She was young, life was gay and hers to enjoy, if she would.

She took the hand Ray held out to her and as they ran up the steps together, she could feel the aqua dress swishing gaily about her.